# DELLA MORTIKA
## THE LIBRARY OF WONDER

# GERALDINE F. MARTIN

ILLUSTRATIONS BY
PAUL J. MARTIN & MARISA MARTIN

VIVID
PUBLISHING

Copyright © 2015 Geraldine F. Martin

Published by Vivid Publishing
P.O. Box 948, Fremantle
Western Australia 6959
www.vividpublishing.com.au

National Library of Australia cataloguing-in-publication data:
Creator: Martin, Geraldine F., author.
Title:     Della Mortika : The Library of Wonder / Geraldine F Martin.
ISBN:      9781925442007 (paperback)
Series:    Della Mortika steampunk adventures ; Bk. 2.
Target Audience: For primary school age.
Other Authors/Contributors:
          Martin, Paul J., illustrator.
          Martin, Marisa, illustrator.
Subjects: Fantasy fiction.
          Missing children--Fiction.
Dewey Number: A823.4

To order further copies or to contact the author,
please visit www.vividpublishing.com.au/dellamortika

# ACKNOWLEDGEMENTS

THANK YOU TO ALL MY FRIENDS, FAMILY AND COLLEAGUES WHO HELPED TO BRING THIS, THE SECOND NOVEL IN THE DELLA MORTIKA SERIES, TO FRUITION. IN PARTICULAR, MARISA WHO PAINTS LOVELY CHARACTERS AND WHO MANAGES TO MAKE EVERYTHING LOOK BETTER THAN BEFORE AND PAUL WHO AS USUAL CAME UP WITH SOME AMAZING DRAWINGS. THANKS ALSO TO SONJA CHANDLER WHO EDITED THE MANUSCRIPT AND TO REBECCA FILIPCZYK WHO PROOF READ THE FINAL.

THANKS ALSO TO ARTS ACT, SCREENACT AND THE MEMBERS OF PROJECT POD FOR CONTRIBUTIONS TO THE ORIGINAL STORY ON WHICH THIS NOVEL IS BASED.

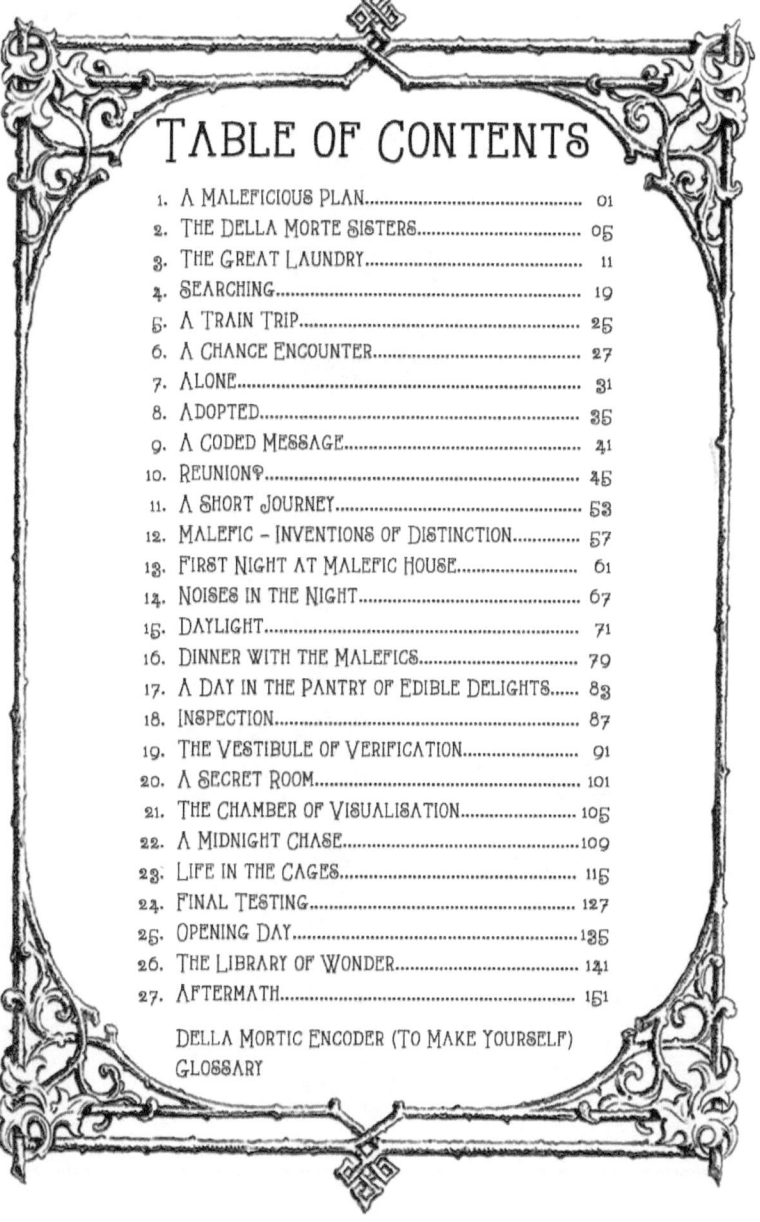

# TABLE OF CONTENTS

# PREVIOUSLY...

...THE DELLA MORTE SISTERS, ABIGAIL, BEATRIX AND ZARAH, SET OUT ON A JOURNEY FROM THEIR HOME IN ENGLAND TO MELBOURNE ON THE VOYAGER SHIP *INVENTION* WITH THEIR PARENTS EDGAR AND CELESTE. ALONG THE WAY DASTARDLY EVENTS OCCURRED WHICH SEPARATED THEM FROM THE PARENTS WHO ARE PRESUMED DEAD BY ALL BUT THE SISTERS. THE GIRLS ARE NOW IN THE CARE OF MRS CROTCHET-SMYTHE, THE SINISTER SUPERINTENDENT OF THE NOTORIOUS SKIPPING GIRL HOME FOR WAYWARD AND HOMELESS GIRLS. AT LEAST, THE SISTERS ARE TOGETHER, BUT FOR HOW LONG?

This is the second novel in the Della Mortika Steampunk Series. The story began in the first novel *Della Mortika – Voyage to the Antipodes.*
www.dellamortika.com

# A Maleficious Plan

T he Melbourne skyline looked like a smudged line of India
ink against the last rays of the setting sun. A pall of smoke and
smog hung over the city dotted with small pools of light
filtering weakly through it from the gas streetlights. Shots of
steam spurted occasionally from holes in the pavements,
evidence of things going on underground. The industrial heart
of the city could be felt throbbing up through the footpaths
ensuring that the residents were always comforted by the
notion that their city was alive, breathing in and out, in and
out, beneath their feet. A lone cable car moved slowly along
Spring Street rocking gently from side to side. The great cable,
which, underground, pulled it along seemed to clank in time
with the beating heart of the city. The cable car driver released
the car from the cable and pulled on the brake and the car
stopped to exchange passengers before it rocked off again
down the road.

Flinders Street Station was still gently lit up. The last trains for the night were at the platforms, patiently waiting for their final clients. Then they would chug out of the city on their way to their suburban stations at St Kilda, Prahan and Heidleberg, among others. Meanwhile, overhead a zeppelin moved ponderously across the sky, its undercarriage lit up, filled with tourists eagerly looking down on the city. They were low enough and close enough to see elegantly dressed couples emerging from the Princess Theatre having just been entertained by Dame Nellie Melba singing Gilda in *Rigoletto*. A couple of street urchins ran past one couple and swiped the woman's reticule off her arm, before skedaddling down Little Collins Street. Her companion shouted and two flying constables, floppers, rounded the corner after the boys. A chase was on and the tourists in the zeppelin were delighted.

A flag attached to the dome of the Exhibition Building announced the 1888 Melbourne Centennial International Exhibition. Two gas spotlights illuminated the flag dimly.

Past the hospital, down Victoria Parade, a light shone in the windows of the annex to a large residential property in East Melbourne. Inside could be seen a figure standing in front of a lectern on which rested a large book.

The figure crystallised into a tall woman who was slowly and intently turning the pages of the book. On her head rested a tiny top hat set at an eccentric angle.

The lectern was placed in front of large windows and bookshelves, the space lit by a gaslight chandelier, which spotlighted the centre of the room. Next to the lectern stood a high table on which was placed a circular device holding a number of elaborately decorated cards. The device was simply a spindle with rotating arms from which hung the individual components. There were five spaces yet to be filled. Alongside was a small stack of cards showing only their backs.

A storm was gathering. Thunder could be heard in the distance and several lightning strikes cut across the sky.

The woman came to the page she sought and threw her arms in the air, laughing triumphantly. The thunder increased and lightning illuminated the room – a library – and above the central window a distinctive crest read: *Malefic – Inventions of Distinction.*

Still laughing, she tapped the page over and over. There was a beautiful drawing in the book of the device on the table, fully laden with cards. The woman picked up the small stack of cards and revealed there were only five there – A, B, Q, X and Z. Throwing her head back she cackled madly and spun the device on the table.

"Oh, father," she cried. "I wish you could see us now."

# The Della Morte Sisters

T hree young girls were huddled together whispering furiously, their heads almost touching. They were seated in the dining room of the Skipping Girl Home for Homeless and Wayward Girls. The tables were trestle type and the walls were covered in signs designed to instil discipline in the residents. Behind their table was one, which read "Wagging Tongues Will Be Removed".

The Skipping Girl Home for Homeless and Wayward Girls was located in the Melbourne suburb of Abbotsford. It was an institution funded by the Victorian Colonial Government's Department of Rectification. It was here that girls from the ages of 7 to 18, who had been found to have no place to live, were housed in return for working in the Great Laundry which provided services to Melbourne hospitals and other institutions.

Suddenly, a bell clanged and the smallest of the three

looked around and quickly back again.

"We should go now," whispered Zarah, the youngest of the Della Morte sisters, "I have Mother and Father's daguerreotype, so I can ask if people have seen them." She put her hand behind the top of her apron and showed a corner of a tiny framed likeness of their parents.

Abigail, the eldest, was quick to reply, "No. Not yet. We have to have a plan first."

Towards the back of the room a large woman was striding along the rows of tables giving a push to the girls who lagged. This was Mrs Blanche Crotchet-Smythe, Superintendent of the Skipping Girl Home for Wayward and Homeless Girls. She came from a family of wealthy merchants who had made their money providing supplies to would-be gold miners. She had been disappointed in love when she was a young woman and carried her resentment with great vigour. She did not know if Daddy had disposed of the profligate Mr Crotchet-Smythe and she didn't want to know. She knew only that she was well rid of him. He had disappeared without trace one day after only six months of marriage. Thereafter, she treated all suitors with complete disdain.

Today, dressed in the latest Victorian style of blouse, bodice, long skirt and bustle she presented a formidable figure. Her grey hair was piled on top of her head to such a height that it tended to sway just out of time with her head. Through it she had thrust a long pin to which were attached several hanging threads of pearls. She would have liked to have attached some bells, but she thought that her movements should be silent, all the better to approach those in her care unheard; some had described her approach as stealthy. Her movements on this day were far from stealthy, however, as she was rounding up the stragglers, for she wanted work to start in the Great Laundry without delay.

Zarah leaned in closer to her sisters and took hold of Abigail's arm.

"Oh, come oooooon, Abigail. We can't wait. The sooner we start looking for Mother and Father the better. Don't you think so, Beatrix?"

Beatrix was the middle sister and the most nervous of the three. She opened her eyes wide and whispered, "Ooooooohhhhh! Yes, I think so too, Zarah. It's so horrible here!"

"Not today, Zarah, we must be cautious. You know what happened the last time you attempted to run away," chided Abigail. She was reminding Zarah that the very first day they were working in the laundry, Zarah had picked the locks on an exit door and run out into the drying yard only to run straight into Ursula McCreedy, the superintendent's right hand woman. She had not been fed until the next morning.

Zarah, a little subdued by this, pulled a stubborn face, but was silent for the moment.

Mrs Crotchet-Smythe was coming closer to the three girls. Ursula, a small, wiry creature jogged along behind her boss and gave a second shove to those Mrs Crotchet-Smythe had pushed, just for good measure. Ursula was wearing long shorts and a tight fitting blue sailor shirt with white collar. On her feet she had long white socks and sandshoes. Her knees were knobbly and stuck out between the long socks and the shorts. Swinging from her belt was an intricately decorated baton and from her neck a brass whistle.

Abigail leaned in, "It's too dangerous to try and escape especially when we have no plan."

Beatrix had been watching the fast approaching Mrs Crotchet-Smythe. "Ooooohhhhh! Perhaps we should wait. Oooowwww!"

As she was speaking Mrs Crotchet-Smythe had finally thumped her way to their table and was standing at the end, while Ursula grabbed Beatrix by the arm and pulled her off her seat. Ursula also grabbed Zarah's arm.

Mrs Crotchet-Smythe slapped her two hands down on the table and bent in to look closely at the girls. Her corset creaked at this unaccustomed movement and her grey beehive hair fell dangerously forward. She frowned and looked at the three girls murmuring almost to herself. "You've been here only three days and already I have your measure." Her purple brocade bodice, trimmed with severe straps and brass buttons, reflected on her face, making her look like she might be in the first throes of a heart attack.

Abigail stood up and tried to smooth things over. "We were just about to get up and ...."

"Save your excuses!" Mrs Crotchet-Smythe bellowed in her broad Scottish brogue. "You Della Mortes are good-for-nothing lazy pistons. Come on! Get moving! There's work to do," she screeched, her voice rising in what can only be described as approaching uncontrolled hysteria. Ursula let go of Beatrix's arm and blew her whistle three times with increasing shrillness as if in sympathy with the rising cadence of her boss's blood pressure.

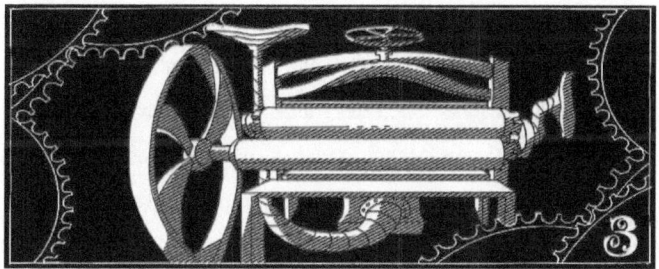

# The Great Laundry

The Great Laundry of the Skipping Girl Home for Wayward and Homeless Girls was a huge cavernous room filled with noise and steam. It was here that most of Melbourne's dirty linen ended up. The linen came from the city's hospitals and grand hotels and the Great Laundry was a part of the BvB corporation of enterprises in the boom town of Melbourne. This type of work was considered suitable for girls as it kept them confined and useful. Soiled linen was picked up all over the city by a fleet of strucksters (steam-powered small trucks) and delivered each morning to the delivery dock at the back of the laundry in large trolley baskets designed for this use. The baskets were then loaded by the laundry girls onto tracks that wound their way around the laundry. Great steam pipes and valves were located along the back wall of the laundry above which the BvB Steam Company logo glowered intently upon the proceedings below.

In one section, girls were pulling linen from the baskets and placing them into the boiling water of the washboard vat. The washboard vat was operated through arms attached to the ceiling mechanical systems, which moved the washboards in a to-and-fro dance. Packets of lye were sitting on the edge of the vats and it was Beatrix's job to ensure that one packet of lye was entered into the vat with each new batch of linen. After twenty minutes of vigorous churning by the washboards she pulled on a giant lever and the dirty water was released through pipes, which eventually emptied into the Yarra River, which ran along the bottom of the Skipping Girl Home's property. The washboards lifted out of the vat and hung in the air like a giant bat and great hooks scooped up the steaming linen and transferred it to a different vat for rinsing. Beatrix then pulled another lever and with a huge whoosh the washboard vat was filled with clean boiling water, ready for the next batch of soiled linen.

Agnes, another inmate of the home, tall and about 18 years old, was in charge of the rinsing vat. She pulled her lever, which sent clean boiling water into her vat. She then oversaw the rinsing which took another 10 minutes and was accomplished by stirring the water and linen with an enormous stick. This was heavy and hard physical work. Agnes had often wondered why her job couldn't be mechanised. She could think of no logical reason for this other than the cantankerous nature of the Superintendent. And it didn't pay to question the Superintendent.

After this a set of huge claws picked up the rinsed and clean linen and deposited it on a large conveyor belt leading to the Great Mangle. It was then up to Abigail, who had learned to time this task with her job on the rinsing vat, and Nerida O'Neill, to smooth out the linen prior to it being squeezed through the rollers of the mangle, removing their arms just in time to miss them being caught between the great rollers.

On the other side of the mangle stood Ching Lan, whose name when translated from Chinese meant "Beautiful Orchid", who was guiding the squeezed linen into a trolley. Ching Lan's family had followed the call of the gold discovered in Victoria in the 1850s and had come to Australia from China to try out their luck, but unfortunately, they had not prospered. Ching Lan had been found wandering the streets of Carlton, lost and alone at 8 years of age. That was three years ago and Ching Lan had grown tough and cynical in the care of Mrs Crotchet-Smythe.

"Hurry up, you two steam puffs!" she yelled at Abigail and Nerida, "You'll get us all into trouble if you're not careful." She leaned in Abigail's direction and snarled, "Believe me your lily white hands will soon be as red and sore as everyone elses".

Abigail recoiled from this as if she had been hit in the face.

She had never been spoken to like this before in her life and she stood staring at Ching Lan in shock. She felt a tug at her arm and turned to look at Nerida who was whispering furiously that they should get the next sheet or they would catch the attention of Mrs Crotchet-Smythe who roamed around the room on her purpose built suspended railway hunting for miscreants and girls not working hard enough. In all the noise and steam of the Great Laundry Mrs Crotchet-Smythe's steam-powered spy-chair (the girls had nick-named it) was very difficult to see or hear and the first the girls knew that they had been targeted was when they felt the sting of an India rubber ball cannoning into their bodies, accompanied by a manic "Got ya!" from Mrs Crotchet-Smythe. This was her favourite supervisory tactic. She fired her balls from a crossbow, which she held at the ready as she steamed around in the swirling space above the girls' heads. The whole set up she called her Panopticoaster.

Abigail was grateful to Nerida who had proved to be a friendly and communicative partner during her first three days in the laundry. Nerida's father had been Irish and her mother had been a member of a local Aboriginal clan. The family had lived in the slums of Richmond until her mother died from tuberculosis and her father drank himself to death.

Other girls were waiting in line behind Ching Lan with empty trolley baskets. When her basket was full she leaned over and straining, as these baskets were heavy, pushed it out the open door into the drying yard. Here her job was to hang the sheets on the lines strung across the drying yard. Huge fans stood in the corners of the yard and assisted the drying process.

At the same time, a girl was coming in from the drying yard and pushing her basket to the edge of the Great Iron Press. A team of six girls pulled the dry linen onto the press and spread it out, snatching their hands and arms away just in time before the burning hot press descended. There was a shot of starch and a spurt of steam applied through the press. The top press plate was raised and the team scooped up the ironed linen and threw it expertly onto the folding table, much like a wool classer throws a fleece onto the classing table.

There was a sign prominently displayed on a central column which stated that it was "5 days since the last fatality" and under that "3 hours since the last injury".

Mrs Crotchet-Smythe was prowling slowly around the room high up on her Panopticoaster. She controlled the speed of her movement with a pedal on the floor of the chair. Across her arms she held her crossbow, which she stroked lovingly. Suddenly, she placed a ball inside the string of the crossbow and wound it back into firing position. She raised the bow and fired a ball at two girls chatting at the folding table. It hit one of them who immediately rubbed her arm and the girls stopped talking.

She fired another ball at Ursula, which hit her on the back of the head. Ursula growled, mumbled and rubbed her head, before trotting over to look up at the Superintendent who pointed to the drying yard through the open door where a couple of girls were wrestling on the ground and Ursula jogged off to take care of the matter, taking up her baton as she went and blowing her whistle.

Later in the morning, there had been a change in responsibilities and Abigail and Beatrix were pushing a trolley basket loaded with soiled linen from the delivery dock towards the first boiler. They passed Zarah who was folding pillowcases at the folding table.

Zarah grimaced and said through clenched teeth so as not to be caught talking, "I know how we can get out of here right now!"

Abigail was shocked, "No, not yet!"

"You're just too scared. You don't really want to get out at all!"

Beatrix quickly intervened, "Yes, we do. It's just that … "

Right then a girl started screaming. Nerida O'Neill had been working on the Great Mangle and her arm had got caught between the rollers. The rollers continued to pull her in until her arm was in up to her elbow. The mechanism was stuck but it still tried to draw the arm through its crushing grasp with regular attempts to keep turning.

Nerida was screaming uncontrollably. Abigail took in the situation immediately, rushed over to the Great Mangle and tried to stop the wheel from trying to turn. She yelled, "Zarah, try to find the release mechanism, hurry!"

Meanwhile, Beatrix had rushed to Nerida's side and was holding her around the shoulders whispering in her ear that it would be all right and they would free her arm any moment now.

Zarah was examining the mangle closely and soon identified a lever close to the floor that she flung back and the rollers opened.

Nerida slumped to the floor in a timely faint with Beatrix cradling her in her arms. Nerida's arm was badly injured and Beatrix was crying and shaking with shock.

Mrs Crotchet-Smythe had been watching proceedings and fired a ball at Ursula who was jogging in from the drying yard and pointed to the mangle. Ursula blew her whistle three times and the doors to the Great Laundry burst open. Two older girls in white coats jogged into the room carrying a stretcher. They loaded the injured Nerida onto it and jogged away out the doors again, Nerida lay still.

From the corner of the laundry, Brodie, a girl with an artificial eye and eyepiece watched the proceedings sadly. Not even an injury could provide you with an escape from the

Great Laundry. Nerida would be fixed up with an artificial arm and she would be back to work in just a few weeks. Brodie's eye had been damaged when she got too close to steam escaping from a hole in one of the pipes.

Ursula organised the clean-up operation, got the mangle going again and pushed the girls back to work. She then jogged over to the injury board and crossed out the "3" and replaced it with a zero. It now read "0 hours since the last injury."

Mrs Crotchet-Smythe reached over her shoulder where her amplifying trumpet was suspended and picked it up. "Back to work, back to work. Valves-a-popping and times-a-wasting, the excitement is over. Back to work," boomed her voice. She then lifted her crossbow and fired a couple of balls at the laggers. Pretty soon, the Great Laundry was in full swing once again.

Abigail and Beatrix returned to their stations and looked around for Zarah. She was nowhere to be seen.

## Searching

$Z$arah was overjoyed that her escape attempt had worked so easily. She pushed up the bundles of clean sheets under which she had hidden and lifted her head above the side of the trolley basket. There was light coming through the windows in the doors at the back of the struckster and she was able to make out the design of the locking mechanism on the inside of the doors.

"Easy steamsy," she said to herself. Her trolley basket was the last one in and so she just leaned over the side of the basket and operated the unlocking bar on the inside of the door. Both doors swung open and Zarah could see the road behind. It was still early so there were not too many people around.

Suddenly, the struckster took a sharp left-hand turn and Zarah's trolley basket went flying out of the back of the van. Zarah grabbed the sides of the basket and closed her eyes. The basket flew through the air and landed upright on the road. It rolled crazily down the road narrowly avoiding two cyclists and a stovercraft before it rolled to the gutter and fell on its side. Immediately Zarah hopped out and ran for cover down a small lane.

When it looked like nobody was going to follow her, she threw her hands in the air.

"Whoo, hoo!" she cried, then quickly pulled her hands down and looked around to take stock of her bearings. She walked a few minutes and came to a street sign telling her that she was in Bouverie Street. Her attention was drawn across the street to a building with the words "Carlton Brewery" suspended above a blue stone archway, as stepping through the archway were four magnificent Clydesdale boilerplate mechahorses drawing a cart brimming with beer barrels. The horses stepped in perfect unison and turned left from the archway into Bouverie Street. Zarah watched and listened to them clip-clopping down the road until they had disappeared from sight.

Ahead of her she could see the Victoria Market buildings and beyond, the city streets. She headed for the centre of town keeping to back streets where her laundry clothes helped her blend in with the population of the inner city, which for the most part was very poor.

This was the first time that Zarah had seen the city other than during that ride in the Constabulary Stovercraft the first day after the three girls were rescued at sea. That day it had been raining heavily and Zarah had not been able to make out much of the detail of the city from under her oilskin sou'wester. Today, however, the rains had gone and the sun was trying valiantly to break through the thick smog that hung over the city.

Melbourne was a boom town, luxuriating in the wealth that Victoria's natural resources provided. She was the Queen City of the South, Marvellous Melbourne and pride of the British Empire. Gold and coal were driving prosperity and the occupants had taken to the steam-driven industrial technology that was being developed across the globe with gusto. The Great BvB Steam Company controlled much of the city's infrastructure from the enormous coal-fired steam and gas station on Flagstaff Hill that could be seen from all over the city. Zarah glanced up and shivered, "Ugh!" she said to herself as she took in the size of the station and the smoke that its towering stacks belched into the air. The power station crouched on the small hill like a spider, ever alert, ever watching. From its boilers steam and gas were pushed out into the city, which eagerly swallowed up as much as its belly could consume. Steam powered the cable cars that traversed the city; provided heat for its wonderful buildings and the homes of the wealthy; and energised the machines of manufacturing and commerce. Gas from coal lit the lights of Melbourne.

Zarah emerged into the main street of Melbourne, Collins Street, and began stopping people in the street. "Excuse me, sir, have you seen these people over the last three days?"

Some people stopped, looked and shook their heads. One said, "They look familiar, but I haven't seen them." Others waved her off as if she was about to put them to some inconvenience. Others again just ignored her, preoccupied with their own thoughts or too lofty to speak to an urchin of the streets, for that is what Zarah looked like. Zarah took no offence but her frustration was mounting.

She entered several shop fronts and asked the shopkeepers the same question. Nobody had seen them or to some of them they also looked familiar.

She entered a lens-maker's shop. It was quite dim inside, the only light coming from a back room from which also emanated a grinding sound. Gradually, Zarah's eyes became accustomed to the low light and she could make out an array of optical equipment that had been beautifully and intricately crafted. There were eyepieces that could be attached to the head, pince-nez which sat comfortably on the nose, monocles that fit nicely into an eye socket. There were also telescopes, large and small and microscopes, short and tall. Light from the back room bounced off the brass and copper structures, which held the lenses. This lens-maker appeared to be an expert metal worker as well as a lens-maker.

Zarah peeped around the curtain to the back room and saw a small man in a white coat with a full brass helmet over which he had placed the most gorgeous set of goggles that Zarah had ever seen. They were decorated with curlicues and scrolls and the straps were held in place with gold buckles.

All of a sudden, the lens-maker lifted his head and Zarah reeled back with the impact of the scrutiny that the metal face had turned on her. He had taken the lens from the grinder and removed his foot from a pedal on the floor. The wheel stopped turning and residual steam escaped with a sigh. He laid the lens on his table and put up his hands to remove his helmet.

Zarah held her breath. "Perhaps I shouldn't have come in here," she thought.

Once the lens-maker had removed his helmet he placed it under his arm. What was exposed was a round face with a friendly smile, "Well, young one, what can I do for you?"

Zarah was so relieved, she hesitated a moment. Then she pulled out her daguerreotype and showed it to the lens-maker. "I am looking for these people. Have you seen them?"

The lens-maker took the likeness and looked carefully at it, turned it over to look at the back and then looked back at Zarah. "No, I haven't seen them." He held out the daguerreotype to Zarah, "But I do recognise them. They are the famous Della Morte inventors, aren't they? I heard that they were coming down here for the Fair at the Exhibition Buildings." He looked carefully at Zarah. "They are missing, you say? I heard they were with v.........." He stopped there and bent over to look even closer at Zarah reaching out his hand to grab her arm, "And what are they to you?"

Zarah backed off but he continued to ask questions shuffling closer to her. She snatched the frame, and bolted out the door and down Collins Street. Her head was reeling with what the lens-maker had almost told her. He knew where they were. And who was 'v...'? Zarah fought the impulse to turn back and question him. That man was far too inquisitive for her liking and she was not at all sure that she could trust him. She was not at all sure whom she could trust in this city.

# A Train Trip

$Z$arah had been showing the likeness of her parents to people all day. She had even showed it to cable car drivers, but no-one had seen them. The only clue she had chanced upon was that the lens-maker had heard they were with "v…" This was not going to plan. Now what should she do?

She was walking along Swanston Street and was about to turn around and head back when she came onto Princes Bridge. From there she could see the railway lines snaking out towards the suburbs. Her mind made up, she headed over to Flinders Street station and surveyed the intriguing boards with their ever-changing lists of destinations. She looked closely at the railway map and located the Skipping Girl Home at Abbotsford near the Yarra River. She quickly found the train that would take her there. She had no money on her; Mrs Crotchet-Smythe having the view that homeless and wayward girls had no need of money. Zarah waited her time then sidled up to a matron with several charges who was entering the platform for the train to Abbotsford and passed through the checkpoint as part of the group.

As the train chuffed into the station at Abbotsford Zarah hopped down from the train before it stopped altogether. Her plan had been to climb the chain wire fence before the stationmaster came out of his office to collect the tickets of the alighting passengers. She found to her dismay that she was the sole passenger to get off the train at that station. The stationmaster spotted her as soon as he opened his door. She was halfway up the fence when he came racing towards her, slamming the station gate as he ran and blowing his whistle furiously.

"Stop, you ticket-evading urchin," he yelled between whistle blows. "Just you wait there till I get to you. Stop! The floppers are on their way, you hear."

Zarah, however, was too nimble and fast and was away before he puffed to a stop and gave up the chase.

# A Chance Encounter

"**G**alloping gears! That was close," Zarah said to herself as she stopped to catch her breath. She tried not to think about the reception awaiting her at the Home, as she was sure she would have been missed by now. She set out walking along the path close to the railway line, which led to the Skipping Girl Home.

Suddenly, she stopped and listened. She could hear a swishing sound coming from somewhere behind her. On turning around she could see in the middle distance two objects flying parallel to the railroad tracks. She knew immediately what these were, rocketeers, or as they were known in Melbourne, floppers. She smiled as she remembered how she had learned this name. It was from a boy the girls met in the holding cells where they awaited an appearance before the Melbourne Magistrate's Court as abandoned and neglected children. "They're coppers. A copper is what we call a member of the constabulary. And these are flying coppers, floppers, see."

Zarah was not keen to be noticed by the floppers, so she ran into an underpass until they flew overhead and disappeared into the distance.

She emerged onto the other side where she saw the brick wall of the railway underpass. This was a wall used for posters notifying of missing persons, army recruitment and upcoming events. A dishevelled-looking man with a roll of posters under one arm and his bucket and brush in the other had just finished putting up one such poster and was moving along the path towards the next station. This poster told of the opening of Professor Octavia Malefic's Library of Wonder to be held in a month's time.

Zarah was reading the posters when slowly a lanky shadow loomed up beside her on the wall in the late afternoon light. It grew and grew and Zarah was preparing to run when she heard a familiar voice. She turned to see the very boy she had been thinking of earlier, Mitchell O'Connor, a somewhat dubious young man of the city. He was well turned out today, complete with jacket, waistcoat and deftly knotted necktie. His boots had been buffed till they shone. He was wearing a black bowler hat and had a monocle firmly nestled in one eye socket.

"You idiot, you scared me nearly cogless," Zarah said

angrily and gave him a push that he absorbed easily, although his monocle dropped to swing on its chain.

"Sorry, Miss Zarah, didn't mean to rattle you. How goes the search for your folks?"

"No luck."

"That's no good, to be sure. And your sisters? How is Beatrix doing?"

"My sisters. Cowards. They want to have a plaaaaaan before they do anything." Zarah placed her hands on her hips. "I left them behind," she growled. She tilted her head, "Why? Why do you want to know?"

Mitchell looked down quickly, his shoulders vibrating slightly and just as swiftly changed the subject. "Will you look at that now?" Mitchell pointed at the latest poster. "I've heard Professor Malefic's library is going to be really something."

Zarah had lost interest in the library and was studying the missing person's posters. "Looks like my parents are not the only ones missing around here," she murmured.

Mitchell replaced his monocle and studied the posters reading some names, "Janine, Kevin, Lenny, Marisa." Nodding his head he said, "These seem mostly sprockets though."

Zarah started to reply when the sound of rocket packs heralded the return of the floppers.

Mitchell's head swung around and when he realised who

was coming he tipped his bowler to Zarah and called as he trotted away, "Valves-a-popping, Miss Zarah! Must go! Good luck to you now!"

Zarah made herself small against the shadows on the wall until the floppers flew by and then she continued walking.

She had walked for a few minutes and then looked over her shoulder thinking that she had heard footsteps behind her; but she saw nothing. The light was fading and the lamplighter was lighting the gas lamps. She continued walking. Now she could really hear footsteps. She started to run. The footsteps became running steps. The owner of the steps was gaining on her. She rounded a corner into an alley way and almost ran into a mechacat that flared up prancing in a sideways stance and hissing and growling ferociously at her intrusion. She screeched to a halt and could hear heavy breathing almost on top of her. Strong hands grabbed her arm and she fell to the ground and looked up to see who had collared her.

# Alone

The Skipping Girl Home was in darkness, except for one upstairs room where the light flickered and spurted. This was Mrs Crotchet-Smythe's sitting room, which was furnished with a collection of timber and brass furniture, including a crystal cabinet on top of which sat a silver tray, crystal decanter and several gleaming glasses. Mrs Crotchet-Smythe was holding one of these glasses half full of sherry. In the other hand, she had a closed parasol with which she was tormenting her mechabird through the bars of its architecturally eye-catching bird cage. She giggled when the bird objected and flew around the cage in circles. Every now and then she reached into the cage and re-energised the clockwork spring by rotating the tail of the bird.

The Superintendent looked up at a sharp rap on the door.

"Come in if you must," she growled.

The door opened and Ursula entered dragging Zarah by the arm. Zarah struggled to free her arm, which resulted in Ursula shaking her vigorously.

"Thank you, Ursula, for bringing our little runaway back to us. You have done well as always," said Mrs Crotchet-Smythe with a little smile for Ursula. Ursula blushed at this and puffed out her chest a little. She let go of Zarah's arm to push her hair back from her face.

Zarah rubbed her arm and gave Ursula one of her black looks, as Abigail called them.

"Now, Zarah, welcome back. We were very worried about you, you know."

"Well, I'm back now and I want to see my sisters."

"I am afraid that is not possible."

At this Zarah looked stubbornly at Mrs Crotchet-Smythe. "What do you mean? Why not? Where have they gone?" she demanded.

Mrs Crotchet-Smythe looked slyly at Zarah with a slight smirk on her square, pudgy face. "If you hadn't run off today you could have gone with them. They've been adopted, and into a very prestigious family – a family of inventors." Mrs Crotchet-Smythe pronounced the word 'inventors' with a reverence usually reserved for mentions of Queen Victoria and Albert.

Zarah opened her eyes wide and her jaw dropped. "What? No, no, I want to go with them. Take me..."

"Be quiet, you little miscreant. Where are your manners? Didn't your parents teach you to speak respectfully to your elders? Not so high and mighty now are you? You with your stories of high-class living and wealthy parents. Oh, that's right, your parents are missing presumed dead, aren't they?

And now your sisters are gone. I would show me a little more respect if I were you." Mrs Crotchet-Smythe's voice had been rising through this tirade, but she stopped suddenly and turned and smiled at Ursula.

"Now, what shall we do with her?" she said quietly, but menacingly, as she turned to her bookcase and ran her finger along *The Discipline and Punishment Manual for Childcare Institutions in the Colony of Victoria, Volumes 1–10.*

Zarah looked over to the Superintendent's desk and noticed an envelope with a distinctive crest in the corner. She bent her head to get a better look, but Mrs Crotchet-Smythe noticed her looking and moved quickly back to the desk and pushed the envelope out of sight.

"Ursula, take her away and lock her in her room."

Ursula did just that, by the three flights of stairs to the attic, and pushed Zarah through the attic bedroom door and locked it.

Zarah moved slowly across the attic bedroom and sat on her bed. She looked around the room. The other two beds were empty.

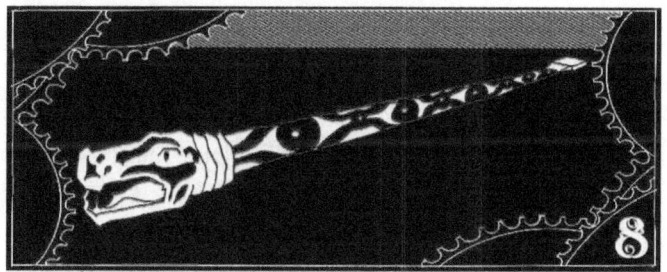

# Adopted

Earlier that day, after Zarah had escaped from the Great Laundry, work had continued until lunch time. Zarah's absence had been noted and Ursula had been tasked with bringing her back to the home.

It was during lunch that Agnes brought Abigail and Beatrix the message that Mrs Crotchet-Smythe wanted them in the parlour. They had been discussing Zarah's escape.

Abigail was contrite, "I should have watched her more carefully. I feel it's my fault that she managed to get away."

"Don't feel that way, Abi," murmured Beatrix in consolation, "You know what she's like. There was no way we could have stopped her today. She was very determined."

It was then that Agnes brought them the message from Mrs Crotchet-Smythe. "Has Zarah been found? Is that why she wants to see us?" asked Abigail excitedly.

Agnes replied with a shrug of her bony shoulders, "I don't know, but you had better hurry. What I do know is that Mrs Crotchet-Smythe has visitors."

Abigail and Beatrix hurried to the parlour. Abigail knocked softly on the door. At Mrs Crotchet-Smythe's "Come in", they entered and Beatrix closed the door behind them.

Mrs Crotchet-Smythe and a man and a woman were standing in the parlour conversing. Mrs Crotchet-Smythe held up her hand to the girls to indicate they were to wait.

"And as I said before, we no longer need a Q or an X; we now need only the A, B and Z," the female visitor was saying.

"Yes, well I have all three. Abigail and Beatrix have just arrived. I am afraid however, both Zarah and Zelda are out for the day."

The female visitor looked unhappy at this news and the male visitor "hurumphed" several times.

The female visitor was tall and slim and bore a great resemblance to her companion. They both had the same hooked nose and large green eyes with thick lustrous black lashes, a rather odd combination of features to be sure. They were in fact brother and sister, twins in fact, Professor Octavia and Dr Octavius Malefic. Professor Octavia wore her black hair in an upswept bun perched high on the top of her head. To the side of this clung a tiny top hat decorated with black netting, which fell over her eyes, slightly, but only slightly, dulling their brilliance. Around her neck hung her goggles. Under her great coat could be seen glimpses of shiny black pants and tall boots, highly decorated brocade vest and frilled white shirt. Her hands were covered in black lace gloves and she carried a small horsewhip, which she snapped against her leg occasionally.

Compared to his sister's elegance Dr Malefic's attire was dry and dusty looking. While Octavia resembled a sleek plum, impatient for life, Octavius was like a desiccated prune, drained and brittle with life's disappointments. His airman's helmet was dusty, his great coat was streaked with grease and oil. His goggles had been lifted up and placed upon his helmet. His hands were bare and he was constantly massaging them one against the other as if to ensure they had not disintegrated. His skin was flaky and dry and his lips cracked. He had the same brilliant green eyes and lustrous black lashes as his sister however. The other trait he shared with his sister was impatience. He was fairly dancing with it, from one foot to the other. He was looking hard at the girls, the girls for whom he had come.

Mrs Crotchet-Smythe turned to the girls. "Professor, allow me to introduce to you Abigail and Beatrix. They have been with us for only a few days but have so far proved to be hardworking and honest. I am sure you will be very happy with them."

"Girls, you are very fortunate to have been chosen by Professor and Dr Malefic to be part of the Malefic family. The Malefic name is one of great importance in today's world. Both Professor and Dr Malefic are great inventors as was their father before them.

Abigail started to speak, but was stopped by Mrs Crotchet-Smythe. "I know what you are going to say. Zarah. Zarah will be joining you tomorrow assuming she returns this afternoon after her day out. Or Zelda, who is at the steamdentrometist today, whoever proves most suitable."

Abigail and Beatrix exchanged glances unsure what this really meant for them and especially for Zarah. Abigail eventually nodded.

"Thank you Mrs Crotchet-Smythe," said Abigail, "may we fetch our belongings and meet the Professor in the hall?"

The Professor spoke before Mrs Crotchet-Smythe could say a word. "Yes, but make tracks fast; I have not a moment to lose."

Abigail and Beatrix left the parlour and ran up to the attic room they shared with Zarah. Once inside Abigail leaned against the door.

"The Malefics!" she said, "They are a very, very famous inventor family. I have heard of them. This will give us a great opportunity to get out of here and into a place where we will be able to start seriously looking for Mother and Father."

Beatrix was packing her meagre belongings into a pillowcase. She turned to Abigail with, "Yes, that's true. But what about Zarah?"

Abigail was thinking hard. "Let's assume that she returns today. I'll leave her a letter and tell her she must do all she can to ensure that she is adopted tomorrow."

"And, then," said Beatrix, "we will all be in a far better place."

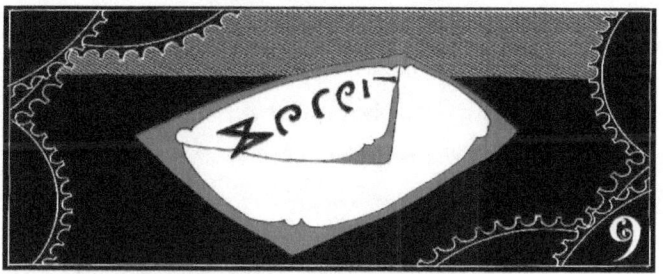

# A Coded Message

Zarah was preparing for bed that night and was lifting her pillow to pull out her nightdress when she saw it.

"Yes!" she cried as she grabbed it. It was an envelope. She ran around the bed to the side table and lit a candle. She held the envelope up to the light and saw it was addressed in code – Dellamortic code – a code devised by Abigail.

"Where is my code breaker?" said Zarah as she looked around the room.

Now Zarah did not have many belongings so it would be difficult for her to lose something as important as her code breaker.

"I know I put it somewhere it would be safe," she said quietly. She thought for a while and then she remembered. She put her hand into the secret pocket she had sewn into the leg of her pants and pulled out a square envelope from which she extracted her code breaker. This consisted of two concentric circles on which were written strange symbols.

Zarah sat down on her bed with the candle on a table beside her. In one hand she held the envelope and in the other her code breaker.

"Now let's see what Abigail has to say," whispered Zarah to herself. She opened the envelope and drew out a piece of paper where there was a page of Dellamortic script.

Zarah had not yet had a chance to use her code breaker so she puzzled over how it all worked.

"Abigail said that there would be a key attached to any message. Now where could it be?" wondered Zarah. "They have to be in the script or on the envelope."

Zarah looked over every surface of the envelope but could find no writing other than the code on the front.

She held the envelope up to the candle and there appeared a very faint line of writing. She held it closer to the candle and the writing darkened. It read, "CC4R – No time for cypher stack".

"Got it," Zarah cried and pulled her tiny notebook and pencil from beneath her pillow.

Zarah twisted the inner concentric circle four places to the right and she had the code deconstructed. She would have had to spend some hours breaking the code without the code breaker.

"Got it," Zarah cried and pulled her tiny notebook and pencil from beneath her pillow.

Zarah twisted the inner concentric circle four places to the right and she had the code deconstructed. She would have had to spend some hours breaking the code without the code breaker.

She scribbled away in her notebook till she had the message decoded.

"Right and tight," said Zarah to herself, "I have to take care of Zelda for a short time tomorrow and then I will be able to join Abi and Bea."

The following day was Sunday when the girls had the afternoon off work and Zarah had plans to make.

# Reunion?

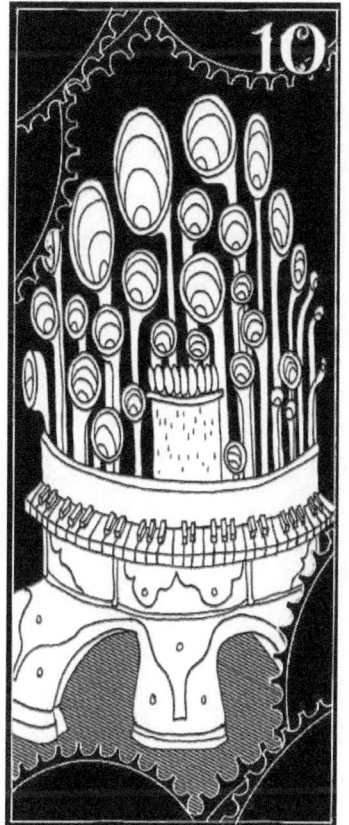

The next evening, Mrs Crotchet-Smythe was sitting in the parlour after dinner idly feeding live flies to her Venus flytrap pot plant. The snap of the trap closing appeared to bring her pleasure and great satisfaction as evidenced by the slight smile and closed eyes it evoked. She kept the flies and other insects in a glass jar alive so that her pretty plant could always enjoy fresh food. Piano music filled the air and then came to a conclusion.

"Play that again, Ursula dear," called Mrs Crotchet-Smythe to Ursula who was sitting at the player piano, the pianola, at the end of the parlour. Nodding Ursula pushed in a button and commenced pedalling again. Her hands rested in her lap for this was a mechanical piano and she turned to her employer to ask, "Did you say that your nephew, trader on the high seas, obtained this fabulous instrument for you, Mrs CS? Where did he get it?"

Mrs Crotchet-Smythe looked a little annoyed at this but answered politely enough, "Don't you worry about where he got it, just enjoy." She looked fondly at a likeness of a young man in a bowler hat, with an elaborate eye piece, which was standing on the side board. "Jack is in town for a few weeks and will be escorting me to the Malefic opening. Such a sweet boy!"

As the strains of *The Delights of an Industrial Paradise* were heard once again Mrs Crotchet-Smythe's head shot up. She rose up and moved to the window.

"Hush, Ursula, I think they're here."

Ursula jumped up and the music ground to a moan and then ended with a sigh.

Mrs Crotchet-Smythe had pulled the curtain aside to see two dark figures alighting from a stovercraft, which was slowly subsiding to the ground with a soft whooshing sound. The slim figure wearing a jaunty tiny top hat tugged on the bell pull near the gates. Mrs Crotchet-Smythe went into the hall and pulled a chain beside the front door, which caused the gates to swing inward, and then she opened the door to receive her guests. Once the visitors were through the gates she pulled the chain twice and the gates closed with a metallic clash.

Ushering the guests into the parlour, Mrs Crotchet-Smythe said to Ursula, "Ursula, fetch the child, will you?" As Ursula jogged off, the two visitors faced Mrs Crotchet-Smythe expectantly.

Professor Malefic addressed Mrs Crotchet-Smythe, "You won't disappoint, as happened earlier, will you?"

"No, no. No. You'll be delighted with her," Mrs Crotchet-Smythe replied soothingly.

At that moment the door opened and Ursula jogged over to Mrs Crotchet-Smythe and whispered in her ear.

Upstairs, in the confined and dark interior of a cupboard where the pneumatic vacuum cleaner was kept, Zelda was wriggling in Zarah's fierce hold. Once Zarah heard Ursula's jogging footsteps fade down the stairs she removed her hand from Zelda's mouth.

"Ow, what do you think you are doing? Dragging me in here and torturing me. My mouth still aches from yesterday, ohhhhhhhhh,' Zelda cried out. She was near to tears.

"Zelda, I'm sorry I hurt you. But I had to stop Ursula finding you. My sisters were adopted yesterday and the people who took them have come back for a girl with a name that starts with Z."

"Owwww," moaned Zelda. "What do I care? My mouth aches so much I just want to go back to bed."

"Great!" said Zarah as she opened the door to see if the coast was clear. "You go back to bed. I hope your mouth feels better soon."

Having established that the corridor was empty, she murmured, "I've got things to do," and headed for the stairs, Zelda already forgotten. Once she reached the bottom of the stairs she sat down on a step outside the parlour to wait.

Meanwhile, inside the parlour, Mrs Crotchet-Smythe was thinking hard. She had wanted to avoid sending Zarah after her sisters, just because she could. However, according to what Ursula had just told her, Zelda was nowhere to be found and she could sense Professor and Doctor Malefic becoming increasingly impatient. She turned to Professor Malefic and said, "Professor, it seems our Zelda is still unwell from her tooth extraction, or should I say teeth extraction as it seems that three teeth were actually rotting in her mouth, and is unable to rise from her bed."

"This is very upsetting news," said Professor Malefic quietly, raising a hand to prevent her brother from advancing on Mrs Crotchet-Smythe, "I hope you have an alternative you can offer us."

Professor Malefic's green eyes turned a steely grey and seemed to bore into Mrs Crotchet-Smythe's violet ones as a screw into a piece of timber. Mrs Crotchet-Smythe closed her eyes to avoid this painful scrutiny and held up her hands as if to defend herself.

"But, of course, Professor, of course we do," she flustered. Turning to Ursula she whispered, "Bring Zarah here, now."

Ursula stepped quickly to the door and opened it. She was about to advance through the door when she stopped and beckoned to someone outside the room and was soon to be seen pushing Zarah into the centre of the parlour. Ursula closed the door.

Mrs Crotchet-Smythe looked over at Zarah and said, "Ah, here she is, our Zarah." To Zarah she indicated the visitors and said, "Professor and Dr Malefic want to meet you, dear."

Zarah stood her ground and looked at the visitors with interest.

Octavius strode toward Zarah and leaning down asked, "Your name is Zarah? Zarah with a Z?"

Zarah nodded.

The Doctor looked over his shoulder and glanced at his sister. She nodded her head. He straightened up and rubbing his hands together said, "Excellent, come on then. Let's go." He turned on his heel and headed for the door.

Professor Malefic took one stride toward Zarah and put her arm around her shoulder.

"Well, Zarah," she said, "I am sure you will be very happy with us. Welcome to the Malefic family."

Mrs Crotchet-Smythe cleared her throat and said with just a

touch of deference, "We need to do the, er, the er, the paperwork, Professor."

Impatiently Octavia stopped, reached into an inside pocket of her coat and took out an envelope with a crest on it. This she pushed into Mrs Crotchet-Smythe's outstretched hand. Mrs Crotchet-Smythe took it greedily.

Smiling, Mrs Crotchet-Smythe said, "Thank you. Thank you. And that other matter, the tickets."

The Professor passed what looked like two event tickets to the Superintendent who asked, "Do you need any more? I have plenty of girls here."

"No, thank you. Zarah will finish off our little family nicely."

Mrs Crotchet-Smythe looked up from fondling her envelope and tickets. "I almost forgot to tell you," she said, "that because Zarah is under 12 years of age, the Inspector of Homes from the Department of Rectificaton will need to visit your home to ensure that she has been taken to an appropriate situation. This will happen in about three days. I'll set it up for you."

"Is that absolutely necessary?" said Professor Malefic, her eyebrows rising imperiously. "Is there nothing we can do to find a way around it?" she continued, nodding almost imperceptibly towards the envelope in Mrs Crotchet-Smythe's hand.

Mrs Crotchet-Smythe's face fell at the possibility of missing out on extra contributions to her bank account, but she managed to say, "Unfortunately, there is nothing I can do. If the Inspectorate found out I had placed a child as young as Zarah without notifying them I would lose my position here. And," she said slyly, looking at the Professor from under her eyelids, "we wouldn't want that, would we?"

"No, that's true. We shall just have to make the best of it. Make the inspection as soon as possible if you would," the Professor stated with a sigh of resignation. She was not one to linger too long on what might have been when her plans were thwarted. She had the flexibility of true genius and was already making alternative plans.

Zarah had been watching the Professor's face closely and thought she could detect some dissatisfaction and impatience. She thought about what being part of the Malefic household would mean to the sisters and she went off cheerily with the Professor.

# A Short Journey

Melbourne at night was dark and dangerous. People kept mostly inside their homes, apart from the few who made their livings, nefarious and otherwise, in the black hours. It was the beginning of spring following an especially cold and nasty winter. It had rained that very night and the streets of inner Melbourne were shining with water puddles and swirling with mists. Gaslights in the streets cast eerie cones of light separated by areas of darkness. Above the city crouched the power station lit up and working all night belching smoke into the darkness. And all the while underground the city throbbed with the beat of its steam-driven heart.

The Malefic's stovercraft glided almost silently through the quiet murky streets. The small steam engines that powered the vehicle were of the Professor's design and the sound of their working was muffled by containment in their own chamber at the rear of the craft. The blades on the fans, which drove the craft forward and pushed air out of the bottom of the craft, and which created the air pressure required to allow it to hover, were feathered on the edges so they made no sound, much like the wings of an owl. The stovercraft moved undetected and hushed, which was just the way the Malefics liked it.

Octavia was at the controls, manoeuvring round corners and under overpasses with great skill. Octavius was seated on one side holding on tightly, his face screwed up and his eyes squeezed shut. He suffered from stover-sickness and endured journeys in the stovercraft because it was his sister's favourite mode of transport and it was difficult to argue with Octavia over things like that.

Both Octavia and her brother ignored Zarah who was seated on the side opposite to Octavius. Sitting next to Octavius and looking up at her unwaveringly was a mechadog the Malefics called Mephistopheles. He was essentially a guard dog and would ensure that Zarah stayed just where she was. Their faith was well placed. Zarah had only to turn her head and a growl would signal that the mechadog was not happy.

Zarah estimated that they had travelled for about 5 minutes when Octavia turned a corner and headed for a large, two-storey house in what looked to her like a well-to-do suburb of Melbourne, possibly East Melbourne. Zarah had made it her business to learn all she could of the City of Melbourne through a map she had found in the room that passed for a library in the Skipping Girl Home. In total there would have been no more than two dozen books in that room, mostly of an "improving" nature. However, on the walls she had found several maps of the city and she had studied them assiduously.

The stovercraft sighed to a standstill. Mephistopheles jumped over the side and loped up to the front door and sat down looking up at the door expectantly.

"Are we home?" the Doctor asked.

"Open your eyes and you'll see that we are," answered Professor Malefic who was holding the controls so that the stovercraft hovered, waiting for the Doctor and Zarah to alight from the vehicle.

Both the Doctor and Zarah stepped out onto the cobbled driveway and Professor Malefic wasted no time in darting off to store the vehicle in the large barn-like structure situated to the left of the house.

The Doctor was swaying slightly and breathing heavily, attempting to quiet the light-headedness and discomfort in his belly caused by the journey.

Zarah took all this in and started to wander off to explore a little. She had taken no more than half a dozen steps when she stumbled to a halt. Sitting on the street in front of her was a snarling Mephistopheles who, his behaviour triggered by her movement, had headed her off. Leaning down she noticed a tiny button in the centre of his chest, but before she had time to explore it closer, which, given the snarls and growls emanating from the dog, she was somewhat loathe to do, she felt her arms taken by a hand on each side, the brother on the right, the sister on the left. The three figures turned as one and headed for the front door, the mechadog bringing up the rear.

# Malefic – Inventions of Distinction

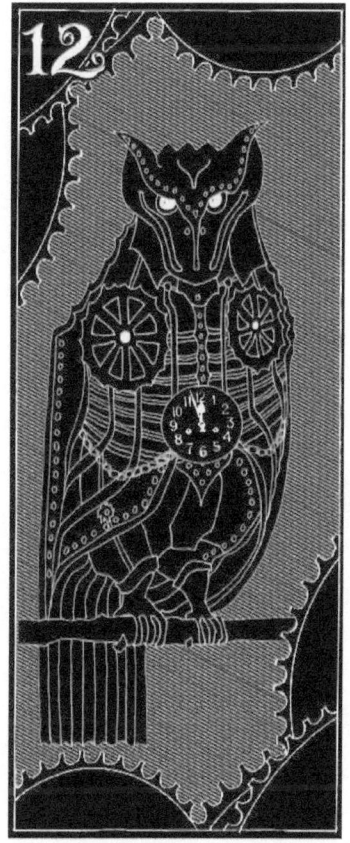

**P**rofessor Malefic slammed the door to the mansion shut and both she and her brother released Zarah who looked around at her surroundings with interest. They were in a large square entry hall or foyer from which three doors led to other parts of the house. Zarah turned around slowly taking in as many details as she could. Above one door was a crest, which was identical to the one on the envelope in Mrs Crotchet-Smythe's office. She was indeed in the Malefic's house.

Under the crest were the words *Malefic – Inventions of Distinction*. Directly opposite the front door on a table, in the place that most households of this size would have a large vase of flowers, a rack for the post and a small silver salver for visiting cards, stood a large mechanical owl, at least 4 feet tall. The owl's head turned in response to sound and followed the conversation that was taking place. Its metallic exterior reflected the gaslight from the wall sconces and shimmered in glorious gold, copper and blue. Embedded in the belly of the owl was a clock. The time was almost ten o'clock and a whirring sound was building momentum from inside the owl. As the minute hand reached the twelve, the wings of the owl lifted and a melancholy "Whoooo" sound escaped from the owl's open beak. This happened ten times.

All three inhabitants of the foyer turned to watch this performance in silence. Zarah was fascinated and continued watching after the owl itself fell silent.

Behind her the siblings were talking while they removed their goggles and coats and hung them on hooks along the wall.

"Octavia, there's not a moment to lose with the library opening imminent. You must test the child and make sure of her suitability," Doctor Malefic said to his sister. The Professor was adjusting her brocade vest so that it sat beautifully and showed off her shapeliness to perfection. She seemed oblivious to the fact that her shapeliness was of no significance whatsoever to the other occupants of the room. She didn't need an audience.

"Yes, yes, of course, Octavius. Don't fuss so. You could worry the wheels off a bogie with your constant chatter. I'll get to it in good time. But all that must wait for a few days until Zarah has settled in and the inspection has passed."

The Doctor, seemingly recovered from his stover sickness, nodded eagerly, "Yes, Octavia. Then father will be proud of us at last."

Professor Malefic rolled her magnificent eyes slightly, "Yes, yes, Octavius. There will be time for all of that nostalgia when the library has opened."

Turning to Zarah, Octavia said impatiently, "Well, child, it's late. We'd better get you to bed. I'll take you up now. You will be under the care of my housekeeper and will be with her at all times. Once thing you must never do, is enter the west wing which is through there, even if she does," she said pointing to the door to the left of the front door. "You must not open that door, ever, do you hear me?"

Zarah dragged her eyes from the owl and stuttered, "Sorry, I, er, I missed that. What did you say?"

"I said," replied Octavia with some impatience, "that you must never enter that door. Understood? Now come this way," she continued and opened the door to the right of the front door. "Come along child!" Zarah followed Octavia through the door while at the same time looking closely at the left door over her shoulder.

"But Professor," Zarah asked. "aren't I going to see my sisters tonight?"

"Not tonight," replied the Professor, "your sisters are away for a few days. There will be plenty of time to see them when they return. Now come along."

Disappointed, Zarah followed the Professor, but she was a little worried. Where were her sisters and where was "away"?

# First Night at Malefic House

Malefic House was large, consisting of three floors and a basement. Once in the hallway outside the entry foyer the lighting was reduced to gas sconces arranged along the walls. This filled the hallway with moving and flickering shadows and lights. Ahead of Zarah, Professor Malefic's leather pants gave off a small squeaking sound as she moved and Zarah caught the faintest smell of cinnamon and cloves, which she attributed to being a favourite perfume of the woman she was following. They went up a staircase and along another corridor till they arrived at a door with a large brass knob and keyhole.

"This was my room when I was about your age, Zarah. I hope you will be comfortable here," Octavia said as she ushered Zarah into the room.

Octavia was looking around the room with a fond look in her eyes. She almost smiled when she took in the train set arranged on a table in the corner.

"This was the first steam engine my father built for me," Octavia said as she pointed to it. "He knew that mechanics and engineering held great interest for me."

"Me, too," said Zarah almost warming to this woman. "I can't wait for the others to come in so we can play with the train set together."

Octavia dragged her eyes away from the train set to look sharply at Zarah. "Others? Other children?" she questioned. "What other children are you talking about?"

"Well, I thought my sis………….." began Zarah, but she was cut off by the Professor saying distractedly, "Of course, your sisters. Yes, yes all in good time."

At that Zarah was silent. What was going on here?

Octavia swept from the room with, "I'll send up the housekeeper, Mrs Bantock, with some supper for you and some night clothes. I'll just lock this door so that you will feel safe and I'll ask her to bring you up a candle. I know what it's like to be left alone in the dark."

Zarah wasn't afraid of the dark and ran immediately to the

door, which was indeed locked. There was enough moonlight coming in through the window to show her that there were bars on it. The eleven-year-old Octavia must have been somewhat of a handful, it seemed.

Zarah was exploring the wall panelling by running her hands over it when there was the sound of a key turning in the lock and a quick knocking. The door opened and standing at the door was a very rotund figure carrying something large on which rested a lit candle. The flickering light from the candle played shadows across the figure's face, which broke into a wide smile when she saw Zarah.

"Well, well, well, it's nice to see a little girl back in this room. It's two decades or more since Miss Octavia was your age and lived in here. I've kept it just as she left it."

Zarah stood watching the housekeeper, waiting for her to move from the door so she could escape through it. But the housekeeper was experienced it seemed at preventing escaping girls and she stood her ground.

"Now, Zarah. It would be best if you would go and sit at your table and I'll bring your supper over to you after I've locked the door again and then you and I can get acquainted."

Zarah knew when she had met her match. She moved to the table and sat down on one of the chairs. Mrs Bantock placed her tray on the chest of drawers near the door, closed the door and locked it with a key, which she wore on the chatelaine hanging around her waist. She then picked up the tray and walked over to the table. She placed a plate of bread and butter in front of Zarah and proceeded to pour two cups of tea.

"Now, that's better. A good cup of tea fixes most things I find, don't you?" said the housekeeper companionably.

"I don't drink tea," said Zarah politely as she ploughed into her bread and butter, "but thank you all the same."

"It was no trouble at all dear," replied Mrs Bantock. "I've brought you some night things and you'll find a jug of water on the wash stand. And of course there is the chamber pot under the bed if you need it."

"May I ask you a question?" enquired Zarah. She took Mrs Bantock's nod for a yes and went on, "Where are the others?"

"Other children? Why child, there are no other children. You are the only child here as far as I know. Now I'll be off. Miss Octavia asked me to lock you in and to leave Mephistopheles guarding your door so that you will feel safe during your first night at Malefic House.

After Mrs Bantock had gone, Zarah ran for the door and tried it. Locked of course, and a snarl and a growl from outside the door assured Zarah that the mechadog was indeed on guard.

Zarah failed to understand the belief here that said that locking children in their bedrooms made them feel safe. Equally strange, the thought of that maniacal, vicious robotic creature guarding her door made her desire to escape from that room and look for her sisters greater than ever. In the end, though, Zarah was a realist. She decided she would go to bed and start more serious explorations in the morning.

Sleep did not come easily to Zarah that night. When she finally did fall asleep she dreamed she could hear her sisters calling for her.

# Noises in the Night

W eak moonbeams were seeping through the window when Zarah was suddenly awake. She lay in her bed listening. A noise had woken her, she thought, but wasn't sure what. Carefully, she looked around the room. There were shadows cast by the moonlight but the room was quiet save for the soft ticking of the clock on the mantelpiece.

Zarah waited.

The clock ticked.

Something moved in the far corner and Zarah held her breath.

It moved again, and Zarah let out her breath. It was just the shadow of the leaves from the tree outside the window moving in the wind.

"Don't be such a steam puff, Zarah Della Morte," she said to herself, "it's nothing but a tree moving outside."

Then she heard it, the sound that must have awakened her.

It was the barking of a dog, muffled but still audible and it seemed to come from the inside of the house. In fact, it sounded like the barking of Mephistopheles.

Zarah was quickly on her feet. If that was the mechadog in the distance then he was not outside her door. She scrambled into her clothes and crept silently to the door. Sure enough there was no sound coming from outside the door even when she rattled the door knob.

Locked doors presented no real challenge for Zarah. She had spent many hours learning about locks and lock picking and she had yet to find a lock that she could not pick eventually. "Oh, this is so easy steamsy," whispered Zarah to herself as she pulled out her lock picking set and a piece of wire she kept in her pocket. "I won't be needing these," she said as she replaced her set of picks back into her pocket. This isn't even a tumbler lock." At home, she had been fashioning her own set of skeleton keys for opening this type of primitive lock but she had not packed them. Instead she had to improvise and bending her wire to the required shape she had inserted it into the lock and was searching for the lever. Feeling the lock give way she turned the knob and slowly opened the door.

It was very dim in the corridor, all the gaslights having been turned right down when the household went to bed. Zarah lifted her head and sniffed. She could just detect the spicy aroma of cinnamon and cloves and she surmised that the Professor had walked this way recently. Zarah remembered the way she and the Professor had taken last night and started to retrace her steps. It was her firm belief that whatever lay behind the forbidden door in the foyer was where she would find her sisters.

Keeping close to the wall panelling Zarah crept quietly and quickly back down the corridor and down the stairs. She passed the dark and silent kitchen and arrived at the door to the foyer. Through the door she heard the whirring sound that heralded the striking of the owl clock. One, two, three hoots she counted. It was 3 am. She was just about to open the door when she heard the shutting of a door and voices. It was the Professor and her brother.

"Should I stay up, do you think, in case something else happens?" inquired the Doctor.

"I've left Mephistopheles on guard. He'll ensure everything stays in order down there. Now, Octavius, you should get some sleep, and so must I. Good night, brother dear." This was from the Professor whose heels could be heard clipping the floorboards and coming closer to the door behind which Zarah now crouched.

The clipping stopped and Zarah took the opportunity to head along the corridor and up the stairs, but she could hear the Professor say snappishly, "This is going to be a long three days but we must keep calm until after the inspection. It can't come soon enough for me." This was followed by a slap, which sounded to Zarah as if the Professor had slapped her leg with her whip.

Zarah was just turning into the corridor to her room when she heard the Professor climbing the stairs smartly. Zarah barely managed to reach her room, shut the door and climb into bed before she heard a key turn and then turn back again three times.

"I thought I ordered Mrs Bantock to lock this door," Zarah heard the Professor say to herself. "I'll deal with her in the morning."

Zarah heard the door knob turn and the door opened. The smell of cinnamon and cloves drifted across the room. Zarah could sense the Professor standing at the door and, noticing that one of her boots was resting just outside the coverlet, slowly moved her foot under on the pretence of turning over slightly in her sleep.

The Professor must have been satisfied that nothing was amiss because she closed the door and locked it. Zarah could hear her heels clicking as she moved down the corridor to her own room.

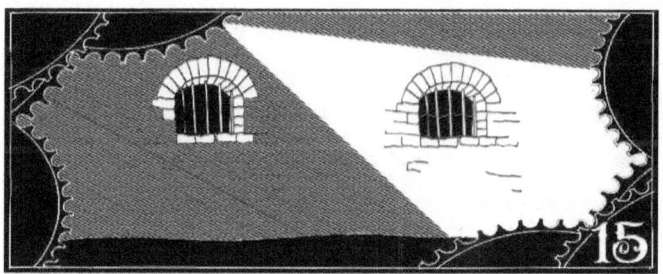

# Daylight

The first Zarah knew of the next morning was when she heard Mrs Bantock unlocking the bedroom door.

"Good morning, to you, my dear," the housekeeper said cheerfully coming over to the bed. "Time for you to rise. Breakfast is ready for you in the kitchen."

The housekeeper went to draw back the bedclothes but Zarah hastily pulled them up to her chin. It wouldn't do for anyone to know that she was fully clothed. This could cause some unwelcome questions about the night before.

"Right," said Zarah. "You go down and I'll be there as soon as I've washed and dressed."

"Independent little sprocket, aren't you? You remind me very much of Miss Octavia at your age. Very well, then, don't lag now as your breakfast will get cold if you do," said the housekeeper as she left the room.

Now that it was daylight, Zarah took her time looking around at the bedroom. To Zarah, it was everything a bedroom should be. It was large and furnished with practical furniture. The walls were covered in wallpaper showing a variety of flying machines – balloons, zeppelins, cam-bikes, flailing ships, jetpacks, all flying over a landscape of steam-age Melbourne. Zarah approved. In the corner was a desk complete with tiny lathe, other metalworking tools and books on engineering. Zarah approved of this also. What she didn't approve of were the bars on the windows. She walked over to the window and looked out onto a courtyard, which in turn led onto a park-like expanse of land. In the medium distance she could see the skyline of Melbourne in the morning sun. She was just examining the window bars closely when she heard her name called from below.

"Zarah, hurry up!" It was Mrs Bantock calling from the bottom of the stairs.

"I'm coming," Zarah called as she left the room and headed for the stairs down to the ground floor.

When she arrived at the kitchen, she found Mrs Bantock alone, standing before the most astonishing kitchen cooking range she had ever seen. It was six feet long and divided into a number of sections. It obviously produced more than just the meals for the family.

"Wow, that is gearsome!" exclaimed Zarah. "How does it

work? What does it do?" demanded Zarah, while she examined closely the dials and pipes and other paraphernalia attached to the range.

"Stand back, child," cried Mrs Bantock. "There are parts of this that are very, very hot and will burn you if you get too close."

"Sit down, now and eat your porridge and I'll tell you all about it," urged Mrs Bantock.

"You see, Zarah, we are outside the limits of Melbourne City and the steam power and gas has not yet reached us here. So we have to produce our own and this is what the Malefic Perfecta Home Energy Production Assemblage does. It was designed by Dr Malefic and will be very popular for outlying and remote homes."

Zarah was entranced by the elegance and sheer size of the thing and wanted to know all about it. Mrs Bantock obliged, "The Perfecta produces all the hot water, heat, steam and gas required to run this house. Dr Malefic is also developing an optional module which will create and store a very new kind of energy, electra something, which they already use in his and the Professor's work."

"Do you mean," interrupted Zarah, "electricity? Are the Malefics working on electricity? Really?"

Mrs Bantock looked taken aback at the fact that Zarah was so incredulous and the look on her face said to Zarah that she felt she had said too much.

Hurriedly, Mrs Bantock continued, "Well that's as may be. You don't want to worry your young head about such things. I will be very busy here for an hour or so. Just sit over there and keep quiet. Here, you can read this with your breakfast."

Zarah took the book from Mrs Bantock. It was the operating manual for the Malefic Perfecta Home Energy Production Assemblage. "Gearsome," said Zarah and opening the manual started to read.

Zarah was deep into the manual when she heard a familiar growl at the kitchen door.

"Ah," said Mrs Bantock. "Mephistopheles is here to look after you while I go into the market." She took off her apron, placed her bonnet on her head and her goggles over that. It was a specially designed bonnet made by herself to fit her goggles, keep her bonnet in place and shade her eyes. Not that they needing much shading these days as the smog hanging over Melbourne blocked the sun's fierce rays on most days. She picked up her basket and left the kitchen with a, "You be good, now, child and don't get into any mischief. You've caused me enough trouble this morning as it is." Zarah suspected the housekeeper had received a dressing down over the unlocked door into her room last night. Zarah felt a twinge of guilt for having caused the situation to occur, but felt justified in that her task was not to have a lovely life as the daughter of the house, but to find her sisters.

Zarah looked through the window to see the housekeeper climb onto her very stylish tricycle and pedal around the corner of the house and off to the market.

Reluctantly, as she was engrossed in the technical details of the Malefic Perfecta Home Energy Production Assemblage, Zarah closed the manual and looked at Mephistopheles lying down across the threshold of the kitchen door. How was she going to give him the slip? She spied the pantry door which was fully boilerplated and was bolted from the outside. Zarah rose slowly and walked across the flagstone floor toward the pantry. Mephistopheles rose and padded (as much as a mechadog can pad) after her. She opened the door and entered followed by the mechadog. Zarah climbed a ladder which was leaning against the side wall and which allowed Mrs Bantock to reach the sherry. She turned to see Mephistopheles standing across the bottom of the ladder. Quickly, she jumped down over the dog to the door. The pantry was too narrow for the mechadog to turn around and he had to back out. Before he could make it through the door Zarah had slammed the door shut and shot the bolt.

Outside in the courtyard Zarah looked around and thought, "Now, where will I start?" She found herself focusing on the forbidden west wing. "There, I think," she said out loud, as she made her way out the back door into the courtyard.

The west wing was larger than the wing where Zarah had spent the night. The walls were of red brick with panelled windows and a slate roof. The roof was pitched, forming a V-shaped gully where the wing met the main house.

Zarah walked up to the walls of the west wing and noticed a row of narrow windows set very low to the ground. She strolled around the end of the wing and found a door set into the wall. She rushed up to the door but found it had no door handle and seemed securely bolted from the inside.

Suddenly, Zarah froze. She could hear what sounded like faint moaning. She followed the sound around the corner to the other side of the wing and the sound strengthened slightly. One of the low windows was open and as Zarah came closer to it, the window moved silently shut. The moaning sound stopped. Zarah knelt down and tried to look in the window but it was dark inside and she could see nothing.

All at once, there was a loud knocking behind her and Zarah turned around to see the Professor standing inside a circular building knocking furiously on the window. The Professor disappeared only to reappear outside the building with a stern look on her face that softened as she came closer to Zarah.

"Zarah," said the Professor obviously attempting to control her anger and speaking through clenched teeth, "I thought I made it clear to you that this side of the house was out of bounds. And where is Mrs Bantock, may I ask?"

"Well, you said that I wasn't to open that door in the foyer. I thought you meant inside, not outside, and Mrs Bantock went to the market," Zarah replied trying to look as innocent as possible. Quickly she stepped around the Professor and pointed to the circular building. "What's that? What are you doing in there? Can I see?"

"That," murmured the Professor softly, looking fondly at the circular building, "is our library. We call it the Library of Wonder." The Professor seemed to come out of a kind of reverie of appreciation and looked down at Zarah. "We are doing renovations at the moment and you cannot come in. It would not be safe."

"I'll be careful. I just want to see ......," wheedled Zarah, but was cut off by the Professor taking her arm and marching her back around the corner to the courtyard.

"I think you had better go back up to your room and stop being so nosy. We will answer your questions at dinner tonight. Now, off you go," ordered the Professor smartly and waited till she saw Zarah enter the back door before she turned on her heel and proceeded back towards the library. The only remorse Zarah felt was that she feared she had once again gotten Mrs Bantock into hot steamsy water.

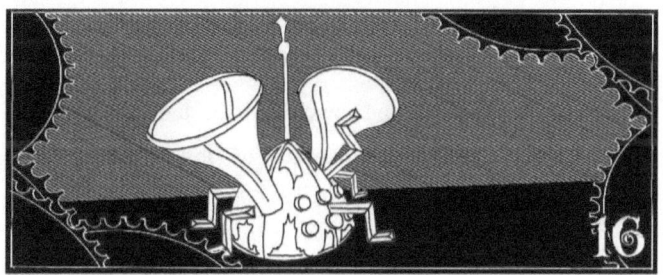

# Dinner with the Malefics

Mrs Bantock served dinner that night in the dining room. This was a splendid room, large, with chandeliers hanging from the ceiling. These were gas fired and the light they gave off flickered and fluttered and cast shadows across the faces of the three people seated at one end of the long cedar table. The glasses were crystal, the cutlery was silver and the china was porcelain. Everything sparkled, and shone, and dazzled.

Dinner was eaten in silence. Zarah, who was naturally chatty, had tried several times to engage her older companions in conversation but each time had been ignored.

Finally, the Professor wiped her lips with her napkin, and laying it down precisely on the table in front of her, said, "Well, I have news for you, Zarah."

Zarah pulled her gaze from her hands where she had been

practicing her shadow puppet poses and looked up at the Professor expectantly.

The Professor's eyes narrowed and she looked directly at Zarah, "Yes, I spoke to the Inspector of Homes today and we have set a time for his inspection."

Zarah blinked and waited.

"He will be here at 3 pm tomorrow afternoon," said the Professor, looking over at her brother who was nodding his head excitedly. "I expect you to behave and answer all his questions politely and in a positive manner. Is that understood?"

Zarah considered for a moment and then asked, "Why are you in so much of hurry? I thought these things took a few days at least."

Professor Malefic pursed her lips at this. "You really are an inquisitive child. The sooner these formalities are over the sooner we can get on with our normal lives."

"But ..." began Zarah.

"There are no buts about it," interrupted the Professor. "It will happen at 3 pm tomorrow afternoon and that's that."

Zarah was silent but she couldn't help wondering just what this really meant for her.

"You will spend all day tomorrow with Mrs Bantock and there will be no wandering around either inside or outside the house. Is that understood?" the Professor asked Zarah.

Zarah lowered her eyes and said nothing.

"Is that understood?" reiterated the Professor, her voice rising with each word.

Zarah raised her head and nodded.

"Good," announced the Professor, "now off to bed with you."

But Zarah was soo..o..o curious she couldn't help herself. She had to ask, "Are you working on electricity?"

The Professor looked up at this and barked, "What did you say?"

"Are you working on electricity? I only ask as I heard that electrical research died with Marconi, Tesla and the others at the World's Fair in Paris," continued Zarah, "and I can see that there are things around the house that need electricity to operate. It's so easy steamsy to see that!"

The Professor, looking at Zarah with something like interest and admiration, leaned over and cranked a handle on a cone-shaped device sitting on the table. Then she pushed a button and waited. There was a label on the cone, which stated proudly "Mistress's Voice One-on-One Communication Device", and under that "A Malefic Invention". There were other labels beside which sat lights, unlit at the moment. A light was flashing against the label that read "Pantry of Edible Delights". Others read, "Vestibule of Verification", "Library of Wonder", "Laboratory of Experimentation" and "Chamber of Visualisation". The light beside the "Pantry of Edible Delights" now shone constantly and a voice could be heard coming from the wire grate covered part of the cone, "Yes, Miss Octavia?" It was Mrs Bantock's voice.

"Come and fetch the child for bed, please, Mrs Bantock. Dinner is concluded," said the Professor after pressing and holding down the button.

The Professor released the button and Mrs Bantock's voice replied, "I'm on my way, Miss."

At this the Professor slammed her finger on the button and said angrily, "Professor! Professor! How many times do I have to ask you to use my proper title?!"

"Yes, Miss. Sorry, Miss. I'll try to remember. It's very hard for me as I've known you since you were a little baby and ......."

"Enough! Come and get the child," said the Professor impatiently and released the button. The light beside the label for "Pantry of Edible Delights" went out.

# A Day in the Pantry
# of Edible Delights

The following day Zarah spent with Mrs Bantock. She was torn between her desire to find her sisters and her desire to investigate and explore the Malefic Perfecta Home Energy Production Assemblage. The realist in her recognised that any attempt at visiting the forbidden areas of the house today would be thwarted by the eagle eye of Mrs Bantock, who, Zarah remembered, had managed to control the questionably behaved young Octavia. Her kindly appearance hid what Zarah decided was a fierce and unquestioning loyalty to the family Malefic. She decided instead to use the day productively to interrogate Mrs Bantock about the Assemblage and even maybe about the goings-on in the west wing.

Mrs Bantock had not been in the kitchen when Zarah had come down escorted by a snarling Mephistopheles who then sat and guarded the door to prevent Zarah leaving the kitchen.

When Mrs Bantock did appear she was pushing a large trolley with empty vats and crumb-filled baskets.

Zarah jumped up from where she had been eating some bread and butter and ran over to the trolley. Mrs Bantock sighed with resignation at seeing Zarah.

"I thought you might come down a little later today," murmured Mrs Bantock, "but I see I was wrong."

"Morning, Mrs B," said Zarah cheerfully, "what have you got there? Where have you been? What have you been doing? Can I come with you next time?"

"Never you mind where I've been and what I've been doing. You ask so many questions you make my mind rattle and squeak like a rusty chain," said Mrs Bantock rubbing her forehead tiredly. She looked as though she didn't think she could stand Zarah's questioning for very long today.

"Here," Mrs Bantock said, pushing the trolley towards Zarah "you can start helping me by cleaning up the trolley while I get on with the day's baking."

So, the day passed, slowly for Mrs Bantock but quickly for

Zarah. Zarah had questions about the steam-cleaning apparatus, the coal-driven gas production module, the reticulated hot water system and the pressurised cooking stove. But it was the electrical module in development that Zarah was really interested in and in the cone-shaped communication device, identical to the one in the dining room, which sat on the end of one of the kitchen benches.

Mrs Bantock endured all these questions quite well really, but was finally exasperated to the extent that she pleaded with Zarah to stop talking and make her a cup of tea.

Mrs Bantock was enjoying her tea when the communicator buzzed stridently. Zarah had been carefully examining the pressure gauge on the oven trying to ascertain how far she could turn the blue dial before something happened, but stopped immediately and ran to the device and pushed the button before Mrs Bantock could rise from her chair.

"This is Zarah Della Morte in the Pantry of Edible Delights. How can I be of assistance to you?" She released the button. She had watched how this thing worked last night at dinner and was fascinated by it.

"Mrs Bantock," said the Doctor's voice, ignoring Zarah, "the Inspector is here. Bring the child to the front parlour, if you would."

"At last," sighed Mrs Bantock, holding out her hand to take Zarah's in hers. With seemingly new-found energy Mrs

Bantock led Zarah out of the kitchen and headed for the parlour.

THE BARON
VON BARBICON

# Inspection

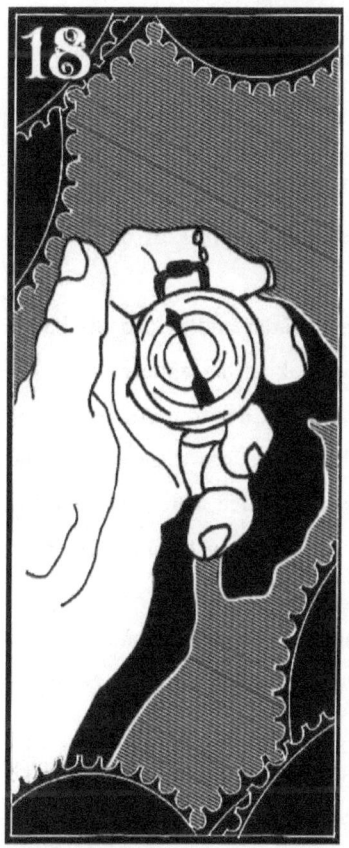

The Inspector of Homes was an avuncular, jolly man with a round and freckled face. His hair was reddish and his eyes blue and he had an amazing moustache, which he had to wax in order to keep its fabulous shape. He often twirled the ends of this magnificence when he was in consideration mode. When in social mode he smiled and nodded constantly. When Zarah entered the parlour with Mrs Bantock she sized him up immediately as a person who would find it very difficult to cross people such as the Malefics and her shoulders drooped a little.

She had been considering during the day how she could

turn this inspection to her advantage. She knew something strange was going on in this house and that she and her sisters were embroiled in it somehow. If she could pass those suspicions onto someone in authority like the Inspector, he might in turn initiate an investigation.

"Inspector," said the Professor walking over to Zarah and taking her by the hand. "May I introduce to you Zarah, shortly to become Zarah Malefic, beloved daughter of the Malefic family."

The Inspector turned to face Zarah and folded his hands across his rotund stomach. He took in her appearance – her straight hair, cut in a bob and fringe, her trousers and boots, her military-style jacket with buttons down each side and particularly her wrist-to-elbow cuff inside which she kept her most secret treasures. Across her front waist hung a chain on the end of which was her pocket watch.

"Well, Zarah, I have only one question for you," the Inspector directed to Zarah, "do you think you will be happy here?"

Zarah hesitated and wondered what to say, when she felt her hand being squeezed by the Professor in what could only be described as a powerful incentive to comply.

"Yes," murmured Zarah reluctantly and was relieved when the pressure eased a little. She looked at the Inspector and winked at him to try and convey her contrary feelings about the matter.

"Good, good, good. You have been given a wonderful opportunity to have a happy and inventive life with the family Malefic. Don't give them any cause for concern," the Inspector said to her as she continued to wink and roll her eyes trying desperately to convey her true feelings.

The Inspector turned to the Professor and said, "Well all seems in order here. Good luck with the child." He looked back at Zarah and observed her closely before turning around and saying quietly to the Professor, "I would have her eyes checked out if I were you. Something seems a little amiss."

The Professor bent down to look at Zarah who of course put on a bland face and lowered her eyes. The Professor saw nothing to concern her and released her hold on Zarah's hand before seeing the Inspector out of the front door.

When she returned, she said to her brother in a satisfied voice, "Well, that's over. Now we can get on with it. Come along child, we have work to do."

# The Vestibule of Verification

The Professor led Zarah out of the parlour into the foyer and turned to take the door to the west wing. Zarah went cooperatively. Wasn't this what she wanted – to know what was going on in the west wing? Well it seemed she was about to find out.

They descended to a floor below and entered a dimly lit corridor. Halfway along the hallway, Professor Malefic stopped outside a heavy door and reaching inside the pocket in her pants withdrew a ring from which hung several keys. Skilfully, she flicked through them and withdrew a large heavy key, which she inserted into the lock in the door and turned. She pushed open the door and entered the room. She lifted her arm and turned up the gaslight on the wall. She called Zarah in and pointed her to a chair in the centre of the room.

The Professor was about to take her own seat when there

was a solid knocking on the door. Frowning, she rose and opened it a fraction. She murmured something to the person in the corridor and turned to Zarah.

"Sit down," she ordered. "I will be back with you soon." Zarah did as she was bid.

Octavia left the room, locking the door behind her.

Immediately, Zarah jumped up and ran over to the door. She tried the doorknob to find that the door was undeniably locked. She dragged the Professor's chair to the door and hauled herself up to the open fanlight above. She stuck her head out of the fanlight and found she could see the tops of the heads of two people. One was the bun of the Professor and the other a man's head, hair slicked down and pulled into a pony tail at the base of his neck. Zarah could see the outline of his top hat under his arm.

"Are the plans ready for construction?" Zarah heard the man say to the Professor.

"Oh, yes. We began construction a week ago. We are tweaking as we go so the final plans will not be available for a while yet," the Professor said.

"And on the other front, the resources, have they all been collected?"

"Finally. The last one, Z, has been confirmed today. I am just about to put her to the test. If she proves suitable then we have a full complement and we can get underway with the experimental trials."

"Excellent, then I will be on my way," the man announced as he bowed to the Professor and turned to leave.

The Professor watched him walking away and then strode after him, catching him at the base of the stair. "I'll see you out", was all Zarah could hear as they climbed the stairs.

Zarah believed she had a few minutes until the Professor returned so she set about exploring the room she was in. She jumped down from the chair and replaced it at the Professor's desk and looked around the room.

Situated directly in the centre of the room was a raised chair. She moved towards it and inspected it closely. A soupcon, a tiny amount, of fear moved in the pit of her stomach at what she observed attached to it. What purpose could this chair serve? There were leather straps attached to the arms, presumably to restrain the arms of the person sitting in the chair, Zarah thought, but why? She looked around again. This wasn't a steamdentrometist's chair was it? It didn't look like one.

Her eyes had moved to an object falling from the back of the chair. This looked like a helmet of some kind with wires sticking out all around its surface. Zarah was just starting to investigate the helmet when she heard the sound of the key being inserted into the lock. She jumped up and ran to the space behind the door. She didn't know what was in store for her but she wasn't sure that she wanted to find out.

Half an hour later Zarah was seated in the chair, her arms restrained and the helmet and goggles on her head. Initially she had refused to cooperate with the Professor, so the Professor had called her brother in to assist. Zarah had been no match for the combined strength of the siblings, so there she was pinned like an insect under a microscope, staring mutinously at the door that had been closed quietly behind Octavius.

The wires from the helmet stuck out all over Zarah's head as though her hair had been struck by lightning. The function of these wires was a mystery. Zarah had no idea what was going to happen to her, but that part of her which was ever-questioning felt a sliver of something close to excitement at the thought of a new technology. She couldn't quite figure out what the technology was but she hoped she would see it in action soon.

Sitting on the right-hand side of the table was a cone-shaped black box with twirling wires emerging straight up from the top. It was similar to the communicator, only much larger. There was a crank handle on one side of the cone and on the other side was a circular hole with a lens inserted into it via a tube, which seemed to be segmented like a telescope. On the wall directly opposite from this box, a white sheet was hanging.

The Professor had been adjusting knobs on the black box and moving the lens in and out. When she was ready she turned to Zarah.

"Now, Zarah, let's begin," said the Professor in a business-like manner.

Zarah dragged her eyes back from the sheet to look at the Professor. The smell of cinnamon and cloves hung cloyingly in the air. From that moment, Zarah couldn't bear that smell. Through her goggles her eyes seemed to glow with rebellion. She said nothing, but her eyes said volumes. She had determined not to cooperate in whatever this activity was. But she was curious just the same.

She didn't have to wait long to find out what it was all about, for the Professor continued, "Now. Zarah. I say a word and you visualise the word in your head. Do you understand?"

Zarah sat motionless.

The Professor bent over, cranked the handle and turned a knob on the black box. A whirring sound started coming from the apparatus and a flickering yellow cone of light from the black box lit up a circle of light on the white screen.

Zarah felt a buzzing in her head and she furiously tried not to think of anything at all.

"Right," said the Professor, "Our first word is 'Zebra'. You must think of a zebra, Z."

Zarah tried to visualize anything but a Zebra. Arcs of

sparks were leaking from the wires on Zarah's head and catching the twirling wires of the black box. There were snapping and fizzing sounds in the air and the faint acrid smell of burning rubber. Zarah's vision had blurred.

The Professor looked up at the screen and waveringly a zeppelin appeared.

"No, no, no. A zebra, Z, a zebra," she cried, exasperated by Zarah's stubbornness.

The Professor rose and snapped the knob on the box to the 'off' position. The arcing sparks ceased. She walked to the front of the chair and lifted Zarah's goggles and she looked deep into her eyes. She whispered directly into her face, her speech chopped and threatening.

"This is your last chance, Z. If you ever want to see your sisters again then you will think of a zebra. You do know what a zebra looks like don't you, Z?"

Zarah nodded. Clarity descended with a thud. The situation was a great deal more serious than she had thought. The Professor lowered the goggles. She returned to her place at the table and snapped the knob on the front of the box to 'on'.

"Very good," she said. "Now, Z, think of a zebra."

Zarah let her mind imagine a zebra, sparks flew, the smell returned and there appeared on the screen a beautiful, bright zebra galloping across an African savannah.

The Professor gave a triumphant shout, "Yes. Excellent.

Moving pictures too! Better than I could have expected and hoped for. You're a natural at this, Z."

She removed the helmet from Zarah's head and the image on the screen disappeared slowly from view. Zarah shook her head and gradually her mind and her vision cleared. She didn't know what had just happened but she thought that it had something to do with the new area of science called electromagnetism and radio waves. She had heard her parents talking about it and knew they too were researching this technology.

The Professor walked over to another corner of the room, to a table upon which sat a circular object studded with elaborately decorated alphabet cards. She picked up the single card lying on the table next to the object. Zarah strained to see over her shoulder and noted that it was a "Z" card. The Professor slotted the "Z" card into the only vacant spot and with her hand spun the object round and round. The Professor stood there with her hands pressed together in front of her breast. She looked very, very pleased with herself.

Suddenly, a strident beeping sounded from the communicator sitting on the Professor's table. The Professor hurried over to the table and pressed the flashing button against "Chamber of Visualisation". Dr Malefic's voice could just be heard above wailing and screaming in the background, ".....trouble ....you'd better come."

The Professor replied, "…yes ….all right ….coming." She looked over at Zarah. "Don't you move. I shall return forthwith." With that she left, locking the door behind her, leaving Zarah alone in the room. Now was her chance and she wasted no time in setting about releasing herself. If there was one thing at which Zarah excelled it was at escaping from tricky situations. She knew she would have to use all her skills to get herself and her sisters out of this one. She started jumping up and down moving her chair toward the table on which she could see the key to her constraints. When she was close enough she kicked the table from underneath. Everything on the table went flying – books, devices and the key to the restraints. Skilfully, she lifted her leg again and kicked the falling key into the air. It fell just out of reach of her open hand and landed on the floor. She rocked her chair over until it fell on its side and she tried to reach the key. She strained and strained, gradually drawing herself closer. At last she grabbed the key and with the one hand managed to unlock the restraint holding her wrists. She quickly unlocked the other restraint and she was on her feet.

She looked around the room and even tried to open the door. It was locked as she knew it would be. As she had done before she dragged the Professor's chair over to the door and pulled herself up until she could stick her head out of the fanlight and confirm that the corridor was empty. She pulled herself up further, climbed through the opening and disappeared. The Vestibule of Verification was empty once again.

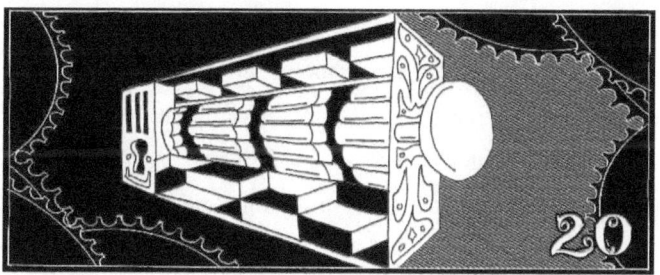

# A Secret Room

Outside the door to the Vestibule of Verification, Zarah landed lightly on her feet, her legs bent to absorb the impact. She scanned the gloomy corridor, lit only by the flickering lights from gas outlets in the wall sconces. In the distance Zarah could hear the muffled sound of a dog barking. Zarah surmised this was Mephistopheles because of the distinctive tone of the bark of the mechadog that she recognised from before.

Keeping to the sides of the corridor, Zarah made her way cautiously towards the sound of the barking. Softly she called out; "Abigail! Beatrix! Are you here? It's me, Zarah."

Suddenly, Zarah stopped. She had heard something. Something from around the corner. There was a pot plant, an aspidistra (a plant often called the Cast Iron Plant for its ability to survive even in difficult conditions) at the corner of a turn in the corridor and Zarah slipped behind it silently as it provided cover for her to see, unseen, what was around the corner.

What she saw was a panel slide back and a door behind it open, through which emerged the Professor, her brother and Mephistopheles. Zarah drew back into the shadows of the leaves of the pot plant and kept very, very still, knowing that even the slightest movement or sound would alert the mechadog to her presence. The Professor pulled the internal door shut and operated an elaborate locking device. Zarah watched the procedure carefully. The Professor then knocked three times on the door and the panel slid shut, the door, and indeed even the opening in the panelling, invisible once more.

Octavia, Octavius and Mephistopheles moved off down the corridor away from Zarah and, turning another corner, disappeared.

In the half dark Zarah stood and started to feel along the panelling, searching for the sliding panel. Her fingers touched a small door with a knob. She dragged the aspidistra under the small door and stood on the edge. This brought her eyes to the level of the knob. She opened the small door and brought her eye up to the opening. What she saw made her fall back in shock. She put her eye up to the hole again and yes, she was able to see the exact same thing, an eye behind one lens of a set of goggles, spinning! Spinning like a pinwheel!

Zarah closed the little door and continued searching for the sliding panel. She soon located it and knocked on it three times. It slid silently back to reveal a heavily fortified inner door to which was attached a hexagonal device decorated with gears and sprockets, knobs and levers. She mimicked the actions that the Professor had done, turn knob two clicks to the right, three to the left, lift the large gear and press the right lever down. She then pushed on the door. Nothing happened. Perhaps she had made a mistake so she tried the same sequence again. Again nothing happened when she pushed on the door. She thought, "Perhaps you have to add the door knocks to the sequence for it to work." So she knocked three times and the panel slid shut. It opened again when she knocked once more. She tried the sequence again. Again, nothing.

Zarah closed her eyes thinking hard. When she opened her eyes she tried again. The Professor had been coming out and she was going in. Back to front of course. She tried the sequence in reverse and the door opened.

Zarah cautiously entered the secret room. It was gloomy inside and she had to wait a few moments until her eyes adjusted to the low light. All around her she could hear small sounds – sniffling, moaning and sighing. And, as everywhere in this place, the faint, cloying smell of cinnamon and cloves. Zarah's nose twitched at this and she tried to suppress the tiny fear in her stomach that the smell generated.

Gradually, as her eyes adjusted to the light issuing from a lamp set on a table situated directly in the centre of the room, Zarah could make out metal bars and padlocks. The room was full of cages!

# The Chamber of Visualisation

Zarah's eyes widened as she looked around the room. The cages were arranged in a circle and inside each was a bed, a chair, a bucket and a helmet with wires sticking out of them, just like the helmet she'd worn in the Vestibule of Verification. Also in each cage was a child. Faces turned towards her with varying looks ranging from fear to indifference. All they could see was a silhouette against the open door. Faint murmurs of "Oh, no" and "Not again" came from the throats of some of the children.

Zarah looked off to her left to where she had seen the

spinning eye. She hurried over to the cage and noticed that it had a "Y" sign above the door. The child in the cage was sitting on the bed looking listless.

"Hello, are you alright?" Zarah asked the child. He stared back at her but said nothing. "Have you seen my sisters, Abigail and Beatrix?" Zarah asked further. Before he had a chance to reply, if indeed he was going to anyway, Zarah heard sounds from the other side of the door.

"Pssst............Psssst .........."

Zarah turned around and saw her two sisters each in her own cage. Abigail in the 'A' and Beatrix in the 'B' cage.

Zarah ran over. "Sockologer! Abigail and Beatrix! Oh, gearsome, I've found you. Let's get you out of here."

She inspected the padlocks and looked around for a tool. She reached into Beatrix's cage and pulled the hair clip from her sister's hair. It snagged as she did this and Beatrix cried out in pain. Zarah ignored her and quickly went to work. "What is this place? What is going on here?" Zarah questioned her sisters as she worked.

Abigail answered her quickly, "Each of the cages has the first letter of our name over the door. That one over there," she pointed to the empty cage with the 'Z' over it, "was for you."

"Well, we'll see about that!" whispered Zarah as she pulled the doors open and headed towards the door. Her sisters started to follow. Beatrix looked around the chamber at the rest of the enslaved children, "But, we can't leave the others ........." she cried in anguish. Zarah turned back but just then running footsteps sounded in the corridor. The Malefics must have discovered she had escaped from the Vestibule of Verification.

Abigail grabbed her sisters and pushed them behind the door. They tried to still their breathing and pressed themselves up against the wall, out of sight behind the door. There were some listless cheers coming from some of the still occupied cages, when the Professor and Octavius with the mechadog ran into the room.

Before the three captors had time to assess the situation the girls scrambled around the door and ran down the hall, Zarah in the lead.

The Professor turned to see their disappearing backs. "Hound! Give chase!" she cried.

# A Midnight Chase

Zarah led the girls down the corridor, up the stairs and through the door into the foyer and out the front door. She could hear shouting from behind her and even more frightening the clipping sound of the mechadog's steel paws upon the wooden floors. Zarah had managed to slow the hound down by closing the doors behind them as they went. Mephistopheles had to wait for Octavia to catch up to open the doors. He had not been programmed to open doors with knobs that required turning. Octavia made a mental note to do so as a matter of priority.

Outside the house, Zarah and her sisters headed towards the

large building to the side of the house, where Zarah had seen Octavia store the stovercraft. It was a cavernous space and housed a number of vehicles. Zarah spied a zeppotrike tethered to the rear of the shed. She pointed to it and the three girls scrambled madly onto the three bicycles suspended below an inflated football-shaped balloon. The Professor had invented the zeppotrike, which used the pedalling of the bicycles to drive the fan that powered the movement of the vehicle, to take herself and guests on joy rides over the city. Tonight it would serve a different purpose.

Meanwhile, the Professor and Octavius had followed the mechadog out of the front door. All three stood in the silence looking and listening for some sign of where the escapees had absconded. The only sound that could be heard was the heavy breathing of the Doctor, who was not as fit as his sister and found all this physical exertion extremely tedious and enervating.

Suddenly, the zeppotrike burst from the shed, the three girls pedalling furiously to drive the fan which moved the vehicle forward. Zarah had her goggles firmly on and she was bending over the handlebars of her bicycle, legs going as fast as she could make them. Once outside the constraints of the shed the zeppotrike started to rise in the air. Abigail, her long skirts pulled up to allow her to pedal, was holding on to her hat with one hand, the other on the handlebar. Beatrix was pedalling also, but her eyes were closed tightly and she was stifling a scream.

The Malefics and the mechadog turned sharply at the sound and started to run towards the shed. The zeppotrike had risen just enough to elude the jumping Mephistopheles who was barking ferociously and snapping his great steel jaws. Zarah kicked out her foot and caught him on the nose. This did nothing to subdue his aggression. If anything, it made it worse.

Once clear of the house and Mephistopheles, Zarah leaned to her left. The sisters followed suit and the zeppotrike banked and made a sweeping turn towards the city.

Five minutes later, feeling that they had escaped the Malefics, the three girls slowed their pedalling and began to enjoy the experience and the spectacle from high above the city. Melbourne had been laid out on a square mile grid of streets with a small amount of suburban sprawl attached to the edges of the grid. To the south of the city lay a large black area. This was Port Phillip Bay, a perfect haven for ships who had braved the rough seas of the Southern Ocean and Bass Strait.

Zarah was looking all around fascinated, when suddenly out of the corner of her eye she noticed something moving on the ground and moving swiftly in their direction. She yelled to her sisters to look and started to pedal faster.

The sight of the stovercraft gaining ground on them was

really something to strike terror in the girls' hearts. The Doctor was driving the stovercraft his goggles holding down his helmet. The mechadog was leaning over the front of the craft, jaws snapping and ears pointed backwards in the wind. In the body of the stovercraft stood Octavia balancing expertly on her strong slim legs and loading up her crossbow with what looked like a steel three-pronged hook.

The closer the stovercraft came to the zeppotrike the more erratic the motion of the girls' craft became. The trike had reached the airspace over Luna Park, a fun park on the edge of the bay and had virtually stopped moving.

"This way!" yelled Zarah leaning to the right, trying to force her sisters to go with her.

"No, that way!" called Abigail leaning to the left, equally determined to lead the group.

"Yes, that way, oh no, this way," wailed Beatrix as she leaned first to the left then to the right. She was pulled in one direction and then another.

"Can't we agree on one direction and all go for it?" cried Beatrix, "we'll never get away if we don't work together!"

The end result of all this prevarication was that the trike made itself a sitting target for the markswoman raising her crossbow towards it.

Suddenly, there was a yank on the wheel of the first bike and the sisters found themselves being turned around and dragged back the way they had come.

"Too, too, easy, steamsy," crowed Octavia to her brother, mimicking Zarah's favourite term that she had used at dinner the night before. The expression on her face morphed from one of smug triumph to one of fury. She turned her face up toward the trike and shaking her fist at the girls, shouted, "I am very cross, A, B and Z. I am very cross indeed."

# Life in the Cages

Dawn was breaking and a sickly yellow light was penetrating into the Chamber of Visualisation through windows high on the eastern wall. Gradually emerging from the gloom and shadows could be seen 27 cages arranged in a circle – one cage for every letter of the alphabet – one cage for every child whose name started with that letter – and one extra with no letter above the cage door.

It was one week after the zeppotrike episode and Zarah had learned at last what was going on in the west wing. The children were being trained to visualise words that they had read to them. They didn't have to visualise every word, only those that started with their name letter. Abigail was responsible for the 'A' words, Beatrix the 'B' words and so on.

Training took place on a daily basis and life had taken on a certain routine for the children in the cages.

Each morning started with the appearance of the housekeeper, Mrs Bantock, who tended to the needs of the children. She had been the housekeeper for the previous Professor Malefic and had stayed on after his death to keep house for his children. She had learned early on in her connection with the Malefics to turn a blind eye to goings-on in the house. She told herself it was none of her business what the Malefics got up to and she made the best of every situation. She had a comfortable life with them and saw the family as her family and the house as her home. Her early entrance into widowhood had led her into a career in service and she was content. Her husband had been destined for a career in the floppers, but his rocket had failed on his first flight and he had fallen to a painful and gory death on the spikes of the fence surrounding the von Barbicon power station. An inquest into the death determined there was no suggestion of foul play and produced a verdict of accidental death. Mrs Bantock started work with the Malefics the very day after the inquest concluded. That was forty years ago and Mrs Bantock had never failed in her loyalty to the family.

Mrs Bantock pushed her trolley through the door and locked it behind her. She then stood arms akimbo and said in a loud and cheerful voice, "Good morning, children. It's time to rise and shine." This was greeted by moans from many small bodies who had been dreaming of better lives than the one in which they found themselves in marvellous Melbourne.

Mrs Bantock liked to have all the children on their feet before she started the day and to ensure this she made an initial tour of the cages running her wooden spoon along the bars stopping at cages of recalcitrants till they dragged themselves out of their beds and stood looking more or less awake.

Each child had a slop bucket in the corner of his or her cage in which to deposit their bodily wastes and the first task every morning was to empty them.

"Right, children," Mrs Bantock said loudly, "you know the drill". She was standing to the left of the door and had her hand on a lever ready to pull it down. As she lowered it, she shouted, "Empty buckets!" In the corner of each cage a circular lid swung open in the floor to reveal an opening into which the children emptied the contents of their slop buckets. Once Mrs Bantock was certain all buckets had indeed been emptied she pushed the lever up and all the lids slammed shut. This activity certainly improved the quality of the air in the chamber.

Aside from their buckets the children had all been issued with a tin bowl, a tin jug, a tin cup and a metal spoon. It was these items that Mrs Bantock required to be kept clean at all times. Failure to do so might result in a reduction of morning rations and as this was the only meal of the day, the children, for the most part, played by the rules. Slow learners regretted their negligence and soon conformed.

Mrs Bantock was the queen of routine and so each morning followed the same pattern. Divergence from routine increased Mrs Bantock's anxiety levels, which could lead to prolonged episodes of crying; such was Mrs Bantock's sadness at such occurrences.

The trolley was loaded up with a large kettle of hot water, a huge pot of steaming porridge, an equally huge basket of fresh bread rolls and a large bowl of nuts and dried fruit. There was also a string bag hanging off the side of the trolley filled with oranges. The smell of the bread alone was enough to make empty stomachs ache with longing. The Malefics believed that they had to keep the children, the cogs in their invention, healthy, as the success of their project depended on active and compliant cogs. Sickness and inability to work by any of the cogs was not in their project plan. However, if any of the cogs failed, there were plenty more orphans out there they could recruit, but the Professor at least was a firm believer in keeping disposal, recruitment and training costs as low as possible. Keeping them healthy was the low-cost option.

Mrs Bantock always started her rounds with the 'A' cage, Abigail's cage. Abigail spoke to Mrs Bantock when she arrived at her cage.

"Good morning, Mrs Bantock," handing her bowl through the opening provided for it.

"Good morning, A," replied the housekeeper, filling the bowl with porridge.

"Please, Mrs Bantock, call me Abigail," said Abigail quietly.

Mrs Bantock's eyes widened and she looked quickly behind her. "Can't; not allowed to", she whispered furtively, "the Professor would have my guts for garters, that she would. You stop that now."

Abigail nodded and accepted her orange, her nuts, dried fruit and hot water from the housekeeper and moved back to her bed.

Mrs Bantock didn't look at Abigail again and pushed off to the next cage, Beatrix's. Beatrix accepted her food and water without speaking. Mrs Bantock continued right around the cages until she reached the last, 'Z', Zarah's cage.

"Hello, Mrs B," chirped Zarah. "Do you know what's happening today? When does the library open? Why don't you call in the floppers? We don't want to be here. Can't you do something?"

Mrs Bantock had grown used to Zarah's questions and demands and while at first they had upset her now she just ignored them. Zarah's frustration was heightened by her hunger, but she accepted her food quietly. The day she had thrown her porridge back at Mrs Bantock stuck in her memory as one she preferred not to repeat. A whole day with water only was not good for a growing girl and she needed her food. Staying alive was essential if she was going to be able to figure a way out of their predicament. And this she was determined to do.

An hour later the Enslaved Children of the Alphabet (this was Zarah's name for them) were ready as usual for that day's morning training session. All the children either stood or sat in their respective cages wearing their helmets with their goggles on or resting their goggles on the front of their helmets. Despite the efforts of the Malefics and Mrs Bantock to keep the children well fed and watered, many were thinner and less healthy looking than when Zarah had first seen them. Several were listless with faces made vacant by their ordeal. Many were crying softly, wiping their noses with their filthy sleeves.

This morning's session was being taken by the Doctor who entered the room with Mephistopheles by his side, snarling and growling as was his wont. The Doctor walked to the centre of the circle of cages to a round table. On the table sat a device that was like nothing the sisters had ever seen before. And they had seen plenty of inventions in their short lives as their parents were famous inventors and they had aspirations themselves in the field. The device consisted of a set of 27 cone-shaped metal components out of the top of which snaked one wire tentacle. 26 of these cones were placed in a circle around a larger cone, which although without a tentacle, dominated the entire ensemble. On the bottom of each cone in the ring was etched a letter of the alphabet. The cones were lined up with their corresponding cages.

"Today," the Doctor began, "we will continue with practising words from *The 2000 Most Common Words in the English Language.*"

He opened the book, placed his pince-nez on his nose, and lifted one hand.

"Boy," he shouted. "Commence pedalling. A to Z, helmets on now."

At this several things happened. A boy in the unmarked cage climbed onto a stationary bike and started pedalling. The children in the marked cages placed their helmets on their heads. One child, 'J' was sitting on the side of his bed with his helmet in his hands. Mephistopheles bounded round to the 'J' cage and barked sharply. The boy 'J' jumped up and placed his helmet on his head as required, tiredly, slowly and without enthusiasm.

The boy on the bicycle increased the speed of his pedalling and the 26 cones opened like a lotus flower with their tentacles facing out to the cages, the tentacle of 'A' pointing to 'A', Abigail, and so on.

"Very well, let us begin," said the Doctor loudly. "JUG," he continued. Then he raced around to the 'J' cage. Jack, the boy in the 'J' cage was concentrating hard and his eyes started to spin like pinwheels.

"JUG, JUG, JUG!" shouted the Doctor, obviously not pleased with progress. The boy on the bike pedalled harder, Mephistopheles barked louder and Jack concentrated more than ever. Suddenly a blinding arc of blue light and sparks flew from Jack's helmet to the tentacle on the cone marked 'J' and the Doctor turned to look closely at the cone. A shimmering image of a jug could be seen faintly on the surface of the cone.

"Better, yes, better than yesterday; you are coming along J", murmured the Doctor.

Thus, training continued for two hours, each of the children taking it in turns to imagine their words and have them appear on their respective cones.

About the time the boy on the bike was ready to collapse, the Doctor looked at his fob watch and called a halt to the session. Gratefully, the children removed their helmets and slumped onto their beds, exhausted every last one of them.

"I will return at 3 pm for the afternoon session, so get plenty of rest between then and now," said the Doctor, matter-of-factly, before turning and performing the lock undoing ceremony and passing through the door. Before the door closed completely, Zarah leaned as far towards the door as her cage would allow her and managed to gain a glimpse of the back of a tall man in a cloak and top hat, standing in the hall.

"Dear me, you're early, ..." began the Doctor before the door closed completely and Zarah could not hear any more of what was being said.

She hurried to the other side her cage to 'Y's' cage to urge him to look out of his peep hole and tell her what he saw. Yardley, however, was sound asleep on his bed, worn out from imagining yachts, yaks and the Yarra.

"Cogs and whistles, that boy is always asleep," complained Zarah. She called across the room to Abigail, "you alright, Abi?"

"Yes, just tired," replied Abigail.

"What about you, Bea?" Zarah called to her other sister.

"I'm tired, fed-up and want to go home. How do you think I am?" grumbled Beatrix from her bed. She turned over and placed her back to Zarah.

Zarah turned her gaze to the back of the room and called out, "Charlie, how are you?"

Charlie was known as Charlie Buttons. It was not his real name. That was Charlie O'Neill. He received his name of Buttons as a result of his obsession with pushing every button he came across. He had got himself into pistons of trouble because of it. He remembered one instance when he had pushed a button on the front of a cable car, which was in actual fact the emergency button that released the cable car hook from the cable, which ran underground and pulled the cable cars around the city. The cable car was heading downhill towards St Kilda Beach at the time. The driver began pulling vainly on the brake, but the out-of-control car ended up in the sea. He had been lucky to get away that time.

Charlie O'Neill was in fact cousin to Nerida who had recently been injured at the Skipping Girl Home for Homeless and Wayward Girls. The Della Morte sisters had not discovered his real name and so Charlie was unaware that his sister had been injured. He had been living with his aunt and uncle, having come down to Melbourne from the Snowy Mountains, and of course, had been orphaned at the same time as his sister and he had ended up in the Melbourne Boys Asylum in South Melbourne where the Malefics had found him. He had pushed every button in the Boys Asylum before he turned 8 with varying results, all extremely annoying for the custodians of the Asylum. These people were only too relieved to have him taken off their hands. He was now eleven and a bright and curious boy.

Charlie was sitting on the side of his bed and called back, "Getting fitter, I think, but not looking forward to another session this afternoon. Have you worked out what's going on here yet, aside from the obvious, that the Malefics are operating some sort of school torture room."

"Well, we know that the helmets are used to transmit our thoughts through a transfer of electromagnetic energy. I don't know exactly how, but I know that practice improves performance."

"Yes, I can see that, but what am I doing pedalling this bike for hours on end. What is that achieving?" asked Charlie Buttons, trying hard to bluff his way through this conversation. He had no idea what electromagnetic energy was.

"I think you are the human energy input into a dynamo or something that produces electricity that drives the cone device."

"But to what end?" came from Abigail, awake now. "What is it all for? We know that research into electricity ended at the bombing at the Paris World's Fair. Could the Malefics somehow be continuing the research in secret? No-one has heard of the research if that is the case. Mother and Father would have mentioned it I am sure."

"That's right, Abi, if the cones are receivers, are they also transmitters? If so where would they be transmitting to, and why?"

They did not have long to wait to find out.

# Final Testing

Outside the chamber the sounds of the morning could be heard faintly. The distinctive clacking sound of the postal cam-driven-flying-bicycle cut through the air sharply as the rider went about delivering the day's mail. Thuds could be heard faintly as parcels and letters went flying down delivery shoots. These riders were expert at finding their targets. Their jobs and their survival depended on it. They were also extremely fit as driving one of the bicycles required enormous physical strength. The working life of a cam-driven-flying-bicycle driver was the shortest of any jobs in the colony. If the strength in their legs failed they fell out of the sky, which usually resulted in death or horrible disability. It was rumoured that the drivers had been meeting in secret to discuss demands for upgrading their machines to the new steam-engine-driven models.

Shouts from the baker announced the arrival of the day's bread, with its accompanying enticing aroma that only fresh bread can give off, followed closely by the milko's delivery. The streets of suburban East Melbourne were coming to life.

Inside the chamber, these sounds were muffled as the walls of the chamber were thick, although the faint smell of the bread did penetrate through the tiny air grates at the top of the walls to the outside. The baker must have walked close to the walls outside that morning because some of the children felt their bellies grumble as they caught a sniff of the bread's hunger-making smell. They didn't bother to shout as they had learned that no sound of the goings-on inside the chamber were audible outside in the street. The Malefics had made quite sure of that.

A shadow passed over the windows of the chamber as the first dirigible of the morning passed silently over the rooftops, blocking the weak sunlight from the room.

The children heard the dreaded three knocks and the clicks associated with the unlocking of the door. They stood up together and held their breaths when they saw who it was, as they had learned to expect the worst of moods from the

Professor, even on a good day.

The Professor accompanied by Mephistopheles entered the chamber carrying what looked like a small pole with a knob on the end. She placed the pole into the top of the central cone of the device on the table and looked at it with a smile on her face. A rare sight for the children and one that Zarah, for one, did not trust. The Professor started to walk slowly around the room looking at each of the children in turn. She returned to the table and stood with her hands behind her back.

"You children," she said gravely, "you should be very, very proud to have been chosen to take part in this, our first practical experimentation of the magnificent Library of Wonder." When she said the words "Library of Wonder" she stood up straighter and pushed out her chest, the words bursting forth with pride and exhilaration.

"So that was what this was all about. The Library of Wonder," thought Zarah. "But how did it work?"

"You can't do this. Someone will come looking for us sooner or later," she cried out.

The Professor looked across at Zarah with something like pity in her eyes. Sorrowfully, she said, "Ah, I don't think so." Tilting her head to one side and raising her eyebrows, she continued, "You see, Z, no-one misses an orphan, do they?" She shook her head slowly, "No-one."

At this, several children moaned and lowered their heads

into their hands. They knew this to be true and were slowly slipping into despair.

Back to business, the Professor turned around to face the table and said loudly, "Now remember, if you betray this moment of greatness by being uncooperative you know what will happen, don't you?"

The Professor pointed to Mephistopheles, who growled on cue and showed all of his shiny steel teeth.

"Don't you?" she demanded once more.

There were a few murmured yeses and nods.

"Don't you?" she cried, her voice rising hysterically.

"Yes, Professor," the children called out in unison.

A crackling voice could be heard emanating from the central cone.

"Octavia, are you ready?" This was Doctor Malefic's voice.

The Professor pressed a button on the central cone, "Yes, yes, Octavius, just a moment," she shouted.

"Boy, start pedalling. Children, helmets on. Now you must imagine your words as the Doctor reads them. Get ready, greatness awaits us!"

Zarah's face suddenly lit up with understanding. "Of course," she said to herself, "the dynamo drives the cones to receive the electromagnetic signals from our heads and the central cone converts them to radio waves to a receiver in the library."

Very clever, she thought admiringly.

"Go ahead," The Professor shouted into the cone, barely able to contain her excitement.

Doctor Malefic's voice started reading, "Giovanni Battista Della Fenestra was a scholar and scientist who lived in Naples at the time of the scientific revolution and reformation. He is also credited with the invention of the steam pressure cooker, which initiated the Italian Industrial Revolution in the mid-16$^{th}$ century."

The Professor had been watching the cones intently. Nothing had appeared except a few scratchy white lines.

The sisters had been trying to resist, but it was very difficult to think of nothing.

The Professor looked around at the cages, "Concentrate! Concentrate!" she shouted at the children. She rushed back to the central cone and leaning in she shouted, "Continue, Octavius."

"It was through his endeavours," continued the voice of Octavius, "that Italy led the world into the industrial revolution initiating the development of many of today's steam-powered marvels such as the Steam Locomotive in 1670 and the Flailing Ship in 1703."

Octavius's voice stopped and gradually pictures of steam locomotives and flying ships appeared. Great arcs of brilliant light had been shooting out of the wires on the children's helmets and linking with the cones' tentacles. The room was ablaze with colour and smoke. The children's eyes were spinning madly and the pictures became stronger and stronger.

The Professor was madly excited. "Does it work? Does it work?" she cried. Her brother burst into the room breathless from having run down from the library. "Yes, yes, the pictures are being broadcast in the library as we speak." Octavius joined in the celebration. He ran to his sister and hugged her. He picked her up in his arms and they polkaed around the centre of the chamber. Neither noticed the heads of the children dropping. Some of the children slumped to the floor heaving. They were spent. The remnants of the arcing and sparking drifted in the air and out of the room through the air vents at the top of the walls.

Breathlessly, the Professor trumpeted, "At last, my magnificent Library of Wonder is complete and ready for presenting to the world. We have proved father wrong, Octavius! He would be so proud of us!" She swirled Octavius once more and said to him as they left the room, "He would be so proud of us! Let us celebrate and raise a glass of sherry to our illustrious ancestor – may he rest in peace."

"So that's what the Library of Wonder is all about," murmured Zarah, "turning words into pictures by sucking out the imagination powers of the brains of children!"

Abigail, Beatrix and Zarah exchanged glances. They too

were spent, defeated and despairing.

Later that night most of the children in the Chamber of Visualisation were sleeping. One of the youngest, a seven-year-old, was crying out for his mama, another was punching an unseen attacker with his tightly coiled fists and yet another turned fitfully in her sleep. The room was dark except for a few wan shafts of moonlight, which crossed the room from the high windows. Close to the door, soft whispering indicated that the Della Morte sisters were not sleeping.

Abigail was sitting on her bed looking first at Beatrix in the cage next to her and then across the room to Zarah.

"We really have to do something," she said softly.

Beatrix was pacing backwards and forwards across the narrow width of her cage. "We're all going to die," she wailed. "I can feel it! I don't want to die. I want to go home and I want to find Mother and Father."

Abigail nodded in agreement and said quietly, "I wish they were here. They'd know what to do."

Zarah was sitting quietly. She was thinking. She pulled the daguerreotype of her parents from her pocket and looked at it sadly. She sighed deeply. She hadn't been listening to her sisters too closely. Just as well, as she became impatient at what she called their "wailing and whining".

After some minutes, Zarah started to nod her head. She said softly, "You know what? I have an idea which might just work." She began to tell her idea to Abigail and Beatrix, her plan. Mephistopheles started to growl. The talking was starting to annoy him.

Zarah stopped talking and turned to the 'Y' cage next door where Yardley was lying on his bed. She whispered her plan to him and he in turn whispered it to Xavier and so it was passed around all the cages, each child woken in turn to join in the plan till it reached Abigail and Beatrix. They both nodded to Zarah in agreement. Whispering continued in an excited fashion, with most children in agreement, although a couple felt it might fail and they would be in worse trouble, until a growl from the hound quieted things and the Chamber of the Enslaved Children of the Alphabet was silent. The children were not asleep however. Bright eyes were shining in the darkness.

# Opening Day

Two days later was the grand opening of the Library of Wonder. Melbourne was abuzz with the prospect of the occasion. Many dignitaries had been invited and many of the important people in the city were coming. The launch of an invention as great as that promised by Professor Malefic was an event at which to be seen. She had of course not disappointed in the past and her reputation was sound throughout the Antipodes and beyond. The Library of Wonder, including their research into radio waves and electricity, however, she had kept strictly to herself, her brother and her patron, the Baron von Barbicon, of BvB

Industries, who controlled the power and steam industry in the colony.

The atmosphere that day was carnival-like. The Malefics had spared no expense. Outside the library there was bunting and balloons. Signs indicated that the Library of Wonder would "amaze, astound and confound you". A brass band played splendid tunes to which the marching girls displayed their talents and skills to perfection. It was as if the circus had come to town.

Sharing time with the brass band was a calliope, a steam organ, which issued forth its own unique brand of flute-sounding music. The calliope master was splendid in his dustcoat and high boots, his highly decorated vest and his top hat. He had four mechanical arms attached to his body which made him eminently suitable to play this particular calliope which itself had two keyboards. His fabulous playing was renowned throughout the colony and beyond. When he played people stopped and not only listened in awe but watched in wonderment at his performance. With his four arms he was able to play the most complex of pieces and even had Melbourne's most popular composer, Nikolai Kavaleski, develop music just for him. He played with passion. He played with his whole body. He played superbly. He threw himself into each piece, his four arms flying through the air, touching down on one or other of the keyboards, his head swivelling as if on a ball and socket, his long red hair sweeping across his face and around his top hat. He was simply magnificent.

In deference to the greatness of the day he wore a bright red carnation pinned to his collar. His eyebrows were thick and his moustache luxuriant. He and his calliope had come to Melbourne not only for this occasion but also to advertise the circus, which was due to arrive in the city at any time. This was *The Antipodean Circus of Oddities and Amazing Sights* and was an annual event in the City of Melbourne. The circus name was emblazoned across the top of the calliope and attracted much interest. The master chatted with the people who stopped and looked and urged them to come to the circus when it came to town.

Members of the public, who had not been invited to the official opening, had turned up in numbers hoping to sample something of the wonder of the occasion. Perhaps they would catch a glimpse of a celebrity, a young inventor, or a person of notoriety. There had been rumours that Melbourne's own great singer, Dame Nellie Melba, had delayed her return to Europe for the occasion. This alas, proved nothing more than a rumour. The origin of the rumour had not been identified, however it had originated about the time that Professor Octavia Malefic had opened the Mechadog Games in August of that year.

Thus, a great crowd of people had gathered outside the

library and these people must be fed, which meant that street food sellers were also present milling around in the crowd selling their wares. The smells of cinnamon doughnuts and fried chips sold in newspaper cones drifted over the scene, as did the aroma of hand-spun fairy floss sold on sticks. Sugar was no novelty to the Antipodes and grew in great abundance in the north of Queensland. It was however, expensive and only a few of those present could afford to buy it.

Security had not been forgotten and four floppers of the Melbourne Constabulary were hovering above the crowd looking out for pickpockets and other petty criminals who would head unerringly to such a gathering.

It was a few minutes before eleven in the morning that invited guests began to arrive. They came in stovercrafts and city balloons and when they stepped onto the carpet leading to the library doors, the crowd issued forth with many 'oohs' and 'aahs'.

Inventors, politicians and professionals, the cream of Melbourne society, proceeded up the carpet to be greeted by Professor and Doctor Malefic and ushered through the doors to take their place inside the library in preparation for the commencement of the demonstration.

Mrs Crotchet-Smythe arrived in a black stovercraft escorted by a tall distinguished looking young man. This was her nephew, her older sister's boy. Her sister had married a man visiting from Eastern Europe and had returned with him to his homeland and had lived there since. The boy was in Australia to gain experience as an army officer her sister had told her.

Among the last to arrive were the Baron and Baroness von Barbicon, the Professor's patron and coal, steam and gas baron of the colony. He controlled vast coal fields in the south-east of the Colony of Victoria and it was his power station sitting atop the hill overlooking Melbourne that produced the steam and gas that powered the city. He supported many inventors in the city, but he managed to keep his personal profile very quiet. He was not often seen at events and so his arrival with his wife was one of especial interest to the public. A hush fell over the crowd, although many made comments on how sickly the Baroness looked. Pale and stooped she appeared to fade beside the magnificence of the Baron himself. Adorned in black from his top hat, to his floating cloak, to his highly polished boots he looked a picture of wealth and affluence. Later, those who had seen him commented on how dark his eyes appeared below his prominent eyebrows and how very thin his lips were. "Not a man to cross," they said.

The Baron and Baroness were greeted by the Professor and Doctor Malefic and the Baroness was ushered inside. The Baron indicated to the Professor that he wanted a word in private.

Quietly, and for the ears of the Professor only, the Baron

asked, "Do you have the blueprints as promised?"

"Of course. Here they are and I am sure you will be satisfied," whispered the Professor.

The Baron took the packet of papers and put them in an inside pocket of his cloak. "I am expecting a successful presentation today and I don't like to be disappointed. I am depending on you," said the Baron to the Professor who replied with a smile, "Have I ever disappointed you in the past?"

The Professor took the Baron's proffered arm and they both strode confidently into the library.

# The Library of Wonder

Inside the Library of Wonder there was an atmosphere of anticipation and expectancy. The library was circular with stacks of books lining the walls. Light came into the library through windows high on the walls. These beautifully crafted leadlight windows created wonderful streaks of colour across the room.

Chairs had been set out in the round and some people were seated already. Others milled around chatting and laughing with friends and acquaintances. Many were looking at the centrepiece of the library, a white screen in a finely carved wooden frame to the side of which stood a lectern on which was placed a large cone-shaped device with a pole extending from the top and a circular lens attachment pointing towards the white screen. The cone-shaped device was embedded into the top of a large and elaborately decorated black hemisphere and was surrounded by 26 smaller cones with tentacles. Steam pipes ran to the device from outlets in the walls and the whole installation gave off the atmosphere of the theatrical. People were bending over to get the best view of the device, trying to figure out how it worked and what it did. The audience was well schooled in the scientific advances of the day; however, this conglomeration was something they had not seen before.

Members of the press had been given front-row seats and were there ready with their pads and pencils. The Melbourne *Argus*'s official newspaper photographer was also present and had already taken some preliminary pictures of the library and the most important people he could find.

At a nod from the Baron, Professor Malefic walked to the lectern and addressed those present.

"If you will all take your seats, we will be able to commence proceedings," she cried loudly, trying to be heard above the hubbub around her.

Eventually people moved to their seats and a hush fell over the library. Mrs Crotchet-Smythe was helped to her seat gallantly by her nephew.

"Welcome, welcome, Lady Governor, special guests and

ladies and gentlemen," the Professor opened grandly. "Thank you for coming to this, what I can only call auspicious, occasion." She looked around, spied her brother smiling at her from the stacks and she smiled and nodded at him.

"Prepare to be amazed. Prepare to be astounded. Prepare to see something the like of which has never been seen before."

The crowd murmured appreciatively.

Doctor Malefic retreated quietly and slipped down the stairs at the back of the library. He had work to do in the Chamber of Visualisation.

"I give you," the Professor said reverentially, closing her eyes and extending one arm towards the screen and other paraphernalia, "The Library of Wonder."

The Professor obviously expected applause and the crowd complied with enthusiasm, although there was some whispering about why she didn't just get on with it.

The Professor must have caught some of these asides because she moved on quickly.

"The illustrious Baron von Barbicon is with us today," the Professor confided in the audience. "You know him as a captain of industry and chairman of our very own BvB Coal, Steam and Gas Power Company."

The Professor glanced at the serious face of the Baron and stated proudly, "But I am here today to tell you that he is also a major benefactor of the Library of Wonder." The Baron bowed his head and gave a little wave when the audience showed their appreciation of his largesse.

"Baron," said the Professor, "may I invite you to be the very first to demonstrate the glorious capabilities of the great Library of Wonder?"

The Baron stood and waited. The Professor continued, "Please, choose a book from the shelves of our Library, any book at all."

The Baron walked to the stacks and reached up and took down a copy of *Great Inventions of the Steam Age*.

"Very good," said the Professor. "Now, proceed to the transposition trumpet and read a paragraph from your book if you please."

The Baron read the words slowly, "One of the greatest inventions of the steam age is the steam locomotive, which hurtles across our landscape at the amazing speed of 50 miles per hour."

The Baron stopped reading and looked up at the screen expectantly.

Meanwhile, down in the Chamber of Visualisation, the children's eyes were starting to spin.

Upstairs in the library, the ring of smaller cones started to spin and scratchy pictures of a steam engine raced across the screen. The words "50 mph" sped after the locomotive. Steam and smoke swirled out of the hemisphere and into the library.

Arcs of blue light and sparks were creating a ring of glorious light.

The crowd in the library stared open mouthed at the screen and the device producing the images. Words had somehow been turned into pictures and were being projected up onto the screen. This was amazing.

"Electrickery!" was whispered and passed around the library. "How can it be?"

They watched for a few minutes before bursting into spontaneous applause. The Professor was pleased. The Baron was pleased. Below Doctor Malefic was pleased as he listened to the applause and the spinning circle of light slowed.

"More, more," cried some members of the audience. The Baron strode to the stacks and retrieved another book, *A Treatise on the Benefits of Burning Coal to Produce Steam.*

He started reading, "Burning coal is the most efficient means of producing steam known to industry."

He looked up at the screen and there could be seen pictures of fire, smoke and steam all emanating from the spinning ring of magnificence in front of the screen.

The Professor's face beamed with triumph. Nothing could stop her now. Her future was secured. She was a great inventor and she had just proved it. Emboldened, she spoke to the Baron's sickly wife.

"Perhaps, Baroness, you might like to try one?" she asked.

The Baroness put her gloved hand to her mouth and nodded. She stood up slowly and the Professor went to her and offered an arm for assistance. Together they walked to the lectern. She whispered into the Professor's ear and she left to retrieve her requested book, *A Day in the Dandenongs* by Miss Pauline Green, a Lady of the Colony. She returned with the book and placed it into the Baroness's hands. The Baroness lifted the book and started to read.

Down in the Chamber, the children were fidgeting with excitement. Abigail, Beatrix and Zarah looked at each other and Zarah jumped to her feet shouting, "Now!!!, Now!!! Now!!!

Upstairs in the library, the Baroness was reading quietly about the prospect of a day in the ferny bush of the Dandenong Ranges. She stopped and looked up at the screen to see the results of her reading. But she saw no ferny forests or winding tracks. What she did see made her gasp and hang on to the lectern to prevent herself from falling.

Downstairs the children's eyes were spinning madly. They were jumping up and down, frantic with the excitement of it all. Doctor Malefic did not understand what was happening and started to scream at them to stop whatever they were doing. He could sense that all was not as it should be but he was confused by the chaos around him.

Arcs of light and sparks were being flung out into the library space. Up on the screen pictures started to appear, a weird kaleidoscope of images as different to the expected "Day in the Dandenongs" as could be. The audience suddenly became quiet as pictures of the Malefic mansion, dark corridors and secret rooms moved across the screen. The sight of a room of caged children with wild looking helmets and spinning eyes horrified them and they gasped at what they were seeing.

The images started to move faster, the cogs and gears of the Library of Wonder machine screamed madly as they revolved faster and faster and steam shot out from under the hemisphere with quickly accelerating force. The arcs of light had gone berserk. The Library of Wonder was no longer a curiosity. It was a beast to be feared. A spinning, out of control, vortex of light, smoke and steam.

The smile on the Professor's face disappeared; her complexion turned a nasty shade of grey; and her eyes bulged at what she was seeing.

The Baron turned to confront the Professor, "Land sakes, Professor! What in a steam-driven paradise is going on? Fix it! Fix it! Before we are all undone."

The Library of Wonder device was now emitting a scream building with intensity every second. The audience members were trampling all over each other trying to reach the door.

They had seen quite enough, thank you. The safety of their persons was now their supreme priority.

Doctor Malefic was running up and down the rows of cages with the mechadog, screaming at the children to behave or they would soon learn the results of disobedience.

The door to the chamber burst open and the Professor took a key out of her pocket and strode menacingly towards Zarah's cage. She reached in and grabbed her by the arm. She dragged her out of her cage and pointed the index finger of her free arm at her, shrieking, "This is all your fault, Z! Father was right; children are useless creatures."

Stepping back from Zarah and releasing her arm she shouted, "Set the mechadog on her, Octavius!"

Octavius crouched down and placed his hand on the back of the hound's head. "Strike! Strike! Strike!" he cried pointing his finger directly at Zarah. Mephistopheles turned to face Zarah, his jaws open, his eyes burning, crouching for a great leap, snarling and growling.

Zarah shot a look at her sisters, before turning back to face the dog. The dog took off from the ground, its great body fully extended and flew through the air towards Zarah.

"Oh, no, Zarah look out!" screamed Abigail.

"Push the button, Zarah, push the button!" yelled Charlie Buttons.

Zarah crouched just in time to miss the terrifying claws

extended towards her and jumped up to poke the dog squarely in the centre of the chest. She stepped aside quickly to avoid the now limp and lifeless body of the dog as it fell with a great clunk onto the floor.

There was silence as the children and the Malefics took in what they had just seen.

There arose great cheering from the Enslaved Children of the Alphabet as they finally realised what had happened.

The Professor took a step towards Zarah, her face red with rage. Zarah stood her ground. As she was reaching out her hands to encircle Zarah's neck, the Professor felt herself pinned by the arms on both sides.

Several curious members of the audience had followed the Professor down the stairs into the chamber and had been observing proceedings. The two floppers also had arrived at the chamber to see what was happening and had flown in to restrain the Professor before she could execute her murderous intentions.

Doctor Malefic, having seen that all was lost, had fled towards the stairs to the library, but was caught mid stride by one of the floppers who promptly turned him around to be marched unceremoniously out of the chamber and up into the outside world.

# Aftermath

Outside the Library of Wonder all was confusion and bustle. The library was in flames and the ringing of bells announced the imminent arrival of the Melbourne Inferno Extinguishing Brigade. The great steam-driven engine almost two-wheeled it around the corner with burly firefighters hanging from the sides, where they stood on the footboards which ran along each side of the engine. More were hanging off the water wagon, which was towed by the engine. In their vibrant red fire-retardant suits the firefighters, or 'Flame Tamers' as the locals called them, jumped down from the engine and wagon even before the vehicles had stopped. Each had a job to do and they quickly set about organising their apparatus. A violent booming noise came from the library followed closely by a huge fireball, which meant the end of the library as the flames engulfed the entire building and were threatening the adjacent Malefic House.

Slowly and steadily a great arm extended from the engine and positioned itself right over the burning building. The crowds loved this bit and they whooped and cried and counted down for the climax. The top of the arm opened like a flower and a great fountain erupted right over the centre of the inferno.

Groups of people stood far enough away from the fire to avoid any flying embers but close enough still to get a good view of proceedings. This was a spectacle not to be missed and which would provide conversational material for days, at least until the next catastrophe happened. This unfortunately would not be too long, as the city of Melbourne was prone to fires and explosions, which comprised the fourth-highest cause of citizen deaths annually. The greatest death rates were from disease, machine accidents and violent crime.

The children, freed at last from the Chamber of Visualisation, were sitting in a group on the ground. The Baroness von Barbicon had organised fresh currant buns and milk to be delivered and the children were all tucking in. Some were too weak to eat and were lying on the ground being comforted by members of the community.

The Malefics were in custody and stood together guarded on either side by floppers who had turned off their jet packs and were standing on the ground.

Professor Malefic had been listening to her brother venting his disappointment and rage at Zarah whom he blamed for the latest disaster to blight his life.

"That Z", he cried shaking his fist at Zarah, "that interfering little rusty sprocket, that miserable excuse for a working cog, that infantile incarnation of a luddite, that little…"

But it suddenly became too much for her and she snapped at him, "Octavius, stop snivelling and whining about that girl." She stopped and looked him in the eye saying more gently, "We'll find another way to prove father wrong about us."

The Baron had had a discussion with the floppers, but had not been arrested by them. He seemed to have convinced them he had no idea that the Library of Wonder preyed on young children and used them as their source of images. He was such a powerful man, it would have taken more than a mere flopper to place him under any sort of arrest.

People were running this way and that. There was much shouting as the fire was brought under control. The calliope master took the opportunity to play music at a frenetic pace from his own composition based on Dante's *Inferno*, his arms and hair swirling frantically, adding to the chaos at the scene and turning it into a fabulous tableau for the still-gathering crowds. He seemed oblivious to the smoke that billowed around him. He was still playing when the flame tamers pushed his instrument further away from the fire.

The three Della Morte sisters had withdrawn slightly from the noise and smoke and were standing near some bushes at the edge of the garden. Charlie Buttons, 'the bike boy', joined them.

Zarah was still excited by the events of the day and was jumping up and down saying, "Well that was gearsomely fantastical! Did you see the look on the Professor's face? She really did mean the mechadog to kill me!"

When she saw Charlie she ran up to him and hugged him. "Thank you for shouting out about the button. I had seen it before and wondered about it. But you were right! And you saved my life. Thank you, thank you, thank you!"

Abigail put her hand on Zarah's arm as if to calm her. "You are right and I am beginning to realise that this city is a dangerous place and we must be more careful."

"Too right, Melbourne's a dangerous place," contributed Charlie. "Stick with me. I know the ropes and pulleys around here."

"Yes, sure," returned Zarah. "You were in as much danger as we were. We have to find our parents. We can't spend time socialising with the locals," she finished teasingly.

"I want to help," said Charlie eagerly.

"Great. We can use all the help we can get," Zarah told him.

"But we can't just stay at that hideous home and hope

Mother and Father will find us," cried Beatrix bravely.

"No, and we won't," replied Abigail thoughtfully. "But we must take things slowly till we learn more about this city and its people."

"Psst, psst," came from the bushes.

The four looked over to the bushes to see Mitchell O'Connor's face through the parted branches. Beatrix leaned in towards the face and said with some austerity, "Well, look who's turned up for the party. You're just a bit late, Mitchell. We are all safe now, no thanks to you."

Just then the Skipping Girl Home for Homeless and Wayward Girls' Stoverbus glided around the corner and pulled up beside the group of children sitting on the ground. Ursula McCreedy jumped down from the vehicle and jogged over to where the Baron and Baroness were standing. At that moment, Mrs Crotchet-Smythe bustled up wringing her hands and wiping her nose.

"How could I possibly have known what was going to happen to my poor, poor girls. You don't think I had anything to do with this?" she asked the little group of people who were gazing at her dispassionately. "Surely not. No of course not," she continued. "These are my girls, my children. I love my children."

Dissatisfied with the lack of response from the Baron and his wife, Mrs Crotchet-Smythe pulled her shoulders back and barked at her assistant. "Ursula, please round up the children and put them on the bus. We will take a detour to South Melbourne and drop off the boys at the Asylum on our way home."

Ursula jogged over to the children and blew her whistle, shouting, "Children, on your feet and march over to the bus." The children stood up, the stronger helping the weaker ones, and moved over to the bus. Ursula stood at the entrance to the stoverbus and counted the children as they boarded.

"21, 22, 23 – four missing! Those duncing Della Mortes!" she cried impatiently and jogged off to find the three sisters and the other one who were not accounted for.

The Baron had overheard Ursula's exclamation and looked startled. "Della Mortes. There are Della Mortes in this group?" he murmured to himself, looking around the crowd, "Where are they?"

The Della Morte sisters and Charlie Buttons were hiding in the bushes by this time with Mitchell O'Connor, who had put his finger to his lips to silence their chatter as Ursula jogged by.

Ursula returned to the bus and reported to Mrs Crotchet-Smythe that they were nowhere to be seen. Mrs Crotchet-Smythe shrugged her shoulders and indicated that they should leave anyway. She and Ursula boarded the stoverbus, Ursula took the controls and the vehicle rose in the air, before gliding smoothly back the way it had come. Mrs Crotchet-Smythe held her hat firmly on her head and the bus disappeared around the corner. Her nephew, with his bowler hat and mechanical eyepiece emerged from behind the stoverbus as it left and strolled towards the Baron.

The Baron watched the bus until it was out of sight before turning to acknowledge the young man. Both tipped their hats and looked thoughtfully at each other. The Baron said quietly, his eyebrows rising slightly, "Well, well. Now that is interesting. I'd like you to keep an eye on those Della Morte girls, Jack." The young man nodded slowly.

Abigail, Mitchell, Beatrix, Zarah and Charlie were huddled together in their hiding place. They were whispering about what they would do now when the sounds of a marching band and the trumpeting of mechaelephants could be heard in the distance. This could mean only one thing at this time of year: the circus was coming to town.

And so it was. The Calliope Master abruptly stopped his playing. He stepped down from the playing platform and closed up and secured his instrument. He then unfolded the driving apparatus from one side of the calliope and he started to drive it slowly away, down the road toward the band music. The steam engine was dual purpose, organ and motor vehicle at the flick of a lever.

Mitchell seeing this, inclined his head towards the

departing musical vehicle, and the others, all previous references to the need for caution and careful planning apparently forgotten, nodded in agreement. Crouching, they ran to the side of the vehicle away from the disaster site and when all danger of being seen was past climbed onto the back of the vehicle, the driver not even noticing them.

*The Antipodean Circus of Oddities and Amazing Sights* was about to have some visitors.

# THE END

*Join the Sisters in their next adventure:*
### *The Carnival of Calumny*
*www.dellamortika.com*

# THE DELLA MORTIC ALPHABET ENCODER

Download from our website (www.dellamortika.com.au) or photocopy this code breaker page onto card. Cut out the two circles. Place the smaller DellaMortic disc on top of the larger English disc and secure with a split pin. Line up A with ☉, then rotate according to the Ceaser Cypher Key. For example, CC6L = Rotate 6 letters to the left. Then translate the Della Mortic code into English.

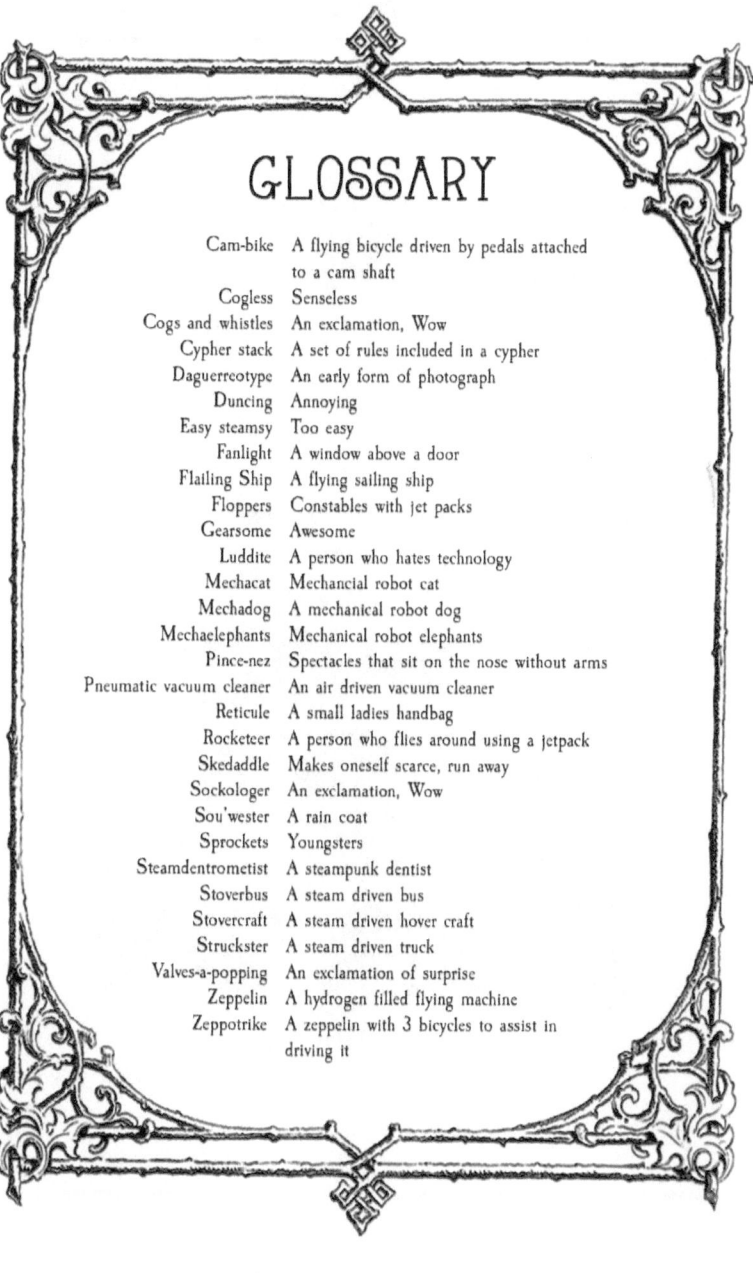

# GLOSSARY

| | |
|---|---|
| Cam-bike | A flying bicycle driven by pedals attached to a cam shaft |
| Cogless | Senseless |
| Cogs and whistles | An exclamation, Wow |
| Cypher stack | A set of rules included in a cypher |
| Daguerreotype | An early form of photograph |
| Duncing | Annoying |
| Easy steamsy | Too easy |
| Fanlight | A window above a door |
| Flailing Ship | A flying sailing ship |
| Floppers | Constables with jet packs |
| Gearsome | Awesome |
| Luddite | A person who hates technology |
| Mechacat | Mechancial robot cat |
| Mechadog | A mechanical robot dog |
| Mechaelephants | Mechanical robot elephants |
| Pince-nez | Spectacles that sit on the nose without arms |
| Pneumatic vacuum cleaner | An air driven vacuum cleaner |
| Reticule | A small ladies handbag |
| Rocketeer | A person who flies around using a jetpack |
| Skedaddle | Makes oneself scarce, run away |
| Sockologer | An exclamation, Wow |
| Sou'wester | A rain coat |
| Sprockets | Youngsters |
| Steamdentrometist | A steampunk dentist |
| Stoverbus | A steam driven bus |
| Stovercraft | A steam driven hover craft |
| Struckster | A steam driven truck |
| Valves-a-popping | An exclamation of surprise |
| Zeppelin | A hydrogen filled flying machine |
| Zeppotrike | A zeppelin with 3 bicycles to assist in driving it |

# Steampunk Emporium

Della Mortika novels and other gearsome steampunk merchandise can be found at the Della Mortika Steampunk Emporium via our website.

WWW.DELLAMORTIKA.COM

# ABOUT THE AUTHOR

GERALDINE F. MARTIN was born in Melbourne and has lived most of her adult life in the Canberra region where she raised three children, worked in public service and designed hats and quilts. These days she writes stories and scripts with her two cats in her studio, which is located right in the centre of her garden in the country. She and her daughter Marisa co-created the Della Morte Sisters and are in the middle of bringing them to life through writing, animation and film. Paul is her son. This is her second novel.

# ABOUT THE ILLUSTRATORS

PAUL J. MARTIN is a trained artist from the Australian National University's Art School as well as a qualified electrician and an Associate Access Consultant. Usually an oil painter, he picked up the pens and pencils to design the gorgeous chapter headings seen throughout this book. Paul has a keen interest in Australian artists and history. He has enjoyed researching the underlying mechanics and engineering in the many machines in the Della Mortika film and those in this book including the Voyager Ship *Invention*. His illustrations based on this research has brought these machines to life.

MARISA MARTIN is a filmmaker, animator and illustrator based in Canberra. Marisa splits her production time between animation and live action projects and has directed leading Australian actors including Noni Hazlehurst, Xavier Samuel, Laura Brent, Gigi Edgley, Inge Hornstra & Paul McDermott. Her films have screened at FlickerFest, St Kilda Film Festival and the New York International Short Film Festival. Marisa took to illustration finding a love in character design. She adores the steampunk world of the Della Morte Sisters and especially enjoys drawing these fabulous girls.